RHYMES WITH FOOL

a novel

Library and Archives Canada Cataloguing in Publication

Courter, Jim, 1947-, author
    Rhymes with fool / Jim Courter.

Issued in print and electronic formats.
ISBN 978-1-988276-21-2 (softcover).--ISBN 978-1-988276-22-9 (PDF)

    I. Title.

PS3603.O87R59 2018   813'.6   C2017-907755-4
                                            C2017-907756-2

PEASANTRY PRESS
Winnipeg, Manitoba, Canada
www.peasantrypress.com

RHYMES WITH FOOL

a novel

JIM COURTER

Peasantry
PRESS

CHAPTER 1

The candidate's wife was blocking my view. Her husband sat in one of the two chairs on the other side of my desk. I assumed she would take the one next to him when I invited them to sit, and at first she did, but soon after Paul Danner began describing the case he wanted to hire me for, she got up and moved around the office. I thought she was merely impatient with his spiel, but it turned into an inspection tour. Not finding much to inspect, she took up a standing position in front of my one window, her arms crossed and her lips pressed together when she wasn't interjecting remarks or corrections.

It was a double-hung window, with each half divided into six smaller panes. Outside it, no more than eighteen inches away, was the red brick wall of the adjacent building. I suppose it never occurred to her that I wanted that view unobstructed, but I did. My building and its neighbor faced east; depending on the time of day, the weather, and the season, the bricks ranged from gray shadow to bright red, about the only esthetic touch in my unadorned office. On that Friday morning in early June, clouds were moving fast overhead, and the light on the bricks shifted dramatically.

Karen Danner was on the tall side, slender and attractive and nicely proportioned. I was just back from a week on retreat with the Trappists, and the Danners were almost my first human contact, so I found their expensive attire and jewelry and hairdos jarring. If the pearls around her throat were genuine, they had to have cost more than my car. I was unsettled, too, to find myself assessing her for her sex appeal so soon after spending a week in a monastery.

Paul Danner was saying, "We haven't heard from Eric since before the end of spring semester, a couple of weeks now, and I'm afraid he's been kidnapped or something."

"He's in college?" I said.

"Yes."

"Where?"

"Marquette. It took him two years after high school to figure out that he wanted to go to college. I'm afraid he made some unfortunate decisions in that time."

"*Unfortunate* is hardly the word," Karen Danner said from the window. "Drugs, the wrong crowd, sexual adventures, you name it." She recited the list like a familiar litany.

Paul Danner held up a hand and gave her a look. "Let me do this, Karen," he said. He licked his lips and squinted slightly, as if to bring his train of thought back into focus. He had square and symmetrical good looks that didn't quite rise to the level of being interesting. Nor did they suggest acuity.

"We live in Brookfield, and we wanted to keep him close," he said. "He went through most of his freshman year at Marquette more or less uneventfully. He even pulled decent grades in the fall and stayed out of trouble. That was all we were hoping for in the short term."

From the window: "If you call mostly Cs decent."

Danner gave a look of resignation, then, satisfied that she was finished, said, "I kept in pretty good touch with him, considering I was tied up in Madison a lot of the time. I came into town every other week or so and took him out to dinner. I tried my best to gauge his spirits and his mood and to discern if he was keeping his nose clean."

Karen Danner took it all in with a look that suggested she had a different version.

"But I was stretched pretty thin, with the campaign and all, and I wasn't able to see him as much as I wanted to."

I said, "Your campaign for the Senate."

"The *United States* Senate," his wife said.

"I'm sure you can understand how time-consuming that's been," Danner said.

I conveyed my understanding with a nod.

"It seemed like things were going well. Then in December, over Christmas break, Eric got into a bad car accident."

"Tell me about that," I said.

"It had been snowing, the streets were treacherous, and Eric ended up sideways and going down an embankment and getting banged up pretty badly."

"He wasn't wearing a seat belt," Karen Danner said. "It's the third vehicle he's smashed up in the last couple of years."

Paul Danner said, "After that it seemed like nothing went right. He healed and returned to school for the spring semester, but then in March he was jumped and mugged near campus. According to his story, four or five black guys pulled up in a car as he was walking to his apartment. They roughed him up and robbed him. He wasn't seriously hurt, but after that, whenever I talked to him, he sounded angry and on edge and afraid. It didn't help that the muggers were never caught."

"When was your last contact with him?"

"Two weeks ago, near the end of spring semester. We talked about his plans. Summer session was one possibility, but I was hoping to put him to work on my campaign. I had in mind something menial for one of my people. I thought it would be a good way to provide him with a job and allow me to keep an eye on him. I didn't want him spending unstructured time."

"That's been a recipe for trouble in the past," Karen Danner said.

"Then when I called him a couple of days later I got his answering machine. I left a message, asking him to get back to me about what his latest thinking was. He never returned my call. He sent me an email saying he still hadn't decided what he wanted to do. It was brief and a little odd, as if we hadn't gone over the issue at all, and he sounded defensive. I got the feeling that he was trying to tell me in so many words to back off and let him decide on his own."

"He used email because he didn't want to have to talk live and explain himself," she said.

"You don't know that, Karen."

She moved from the window and stood behind his right shoulder.

"I didn't immediately follow up because I was busy," he said, "and I didn't want Eric to think I was hounding him. That's proven counterproductive in the past. But it's been two weeks now since we've been in touch, and I have reason to believe he has moved out of his apartment, at least temporarily. I've checked places he might have gone to—people on my side of the family and some of his friends that I know—but nobody I've spoken to has heard from him."

Karen Danner winced when he mentioned his side of the family.

He set a manila envelope on the desk that had been on his lap.

"In there is a copy of Eric's senior yearbook picture from high school. It's posed, and the last time I saw him he had grown some facial hair, but it's as recent a photo as we have."

I opened the envelope and pulled out a color five-by-seven glossy. Eric Danner had dark hair and was thin in the face. In most ways he looked like an ordinary high school senior, although maybe a little more than ordinarily unsettled, lost, and insecure. And something about the eyes and the set of the mouth suggested resentment, maybe even trouble looking for a place to happen.

Karen Danner took the seat next to her husband.

"Height and build?" I said.

"Very close to mine," Danner said. "Around six feet, a hundred-sixty pounds."

"This is a terrible distraction," she said, leaning forward. She seemed to have softened, or to want me to think she had. "If this goes in the wrong direction it could derail Paul's chances for being elected to the Senate."

I had a hunch and decided to play it, in part to see how she would respond. "Are you Eric's mother?" I said to her.

She sat back and looked at me.

Paul Danner said, "Karen is Eric's step-mother."

She made a face. "I despise that term."

"Eric's mother and I divorced when Eric was fourteen."

I said to her, "Did you and Eric get along?"

She responded in even tones. "Sometimes we got along like stepson and stepmother, to use that awful term, sometimes like friends, although never very close ones."

Danner said, "The larger issue is Eric's instability in the past few years. His disappearance has nothing to do with Karen."

To Paul Danner I said, "When you checked with your relatives, did that include your first wife, Eric's mom?"

Karen Danner's face tightened. Her husband said, "No." He paused and thought for a moment. "To be frank, I blame much of Eric's problems on Frieda. She was not a loving mother, or a loving wife, for that matter, and yet when we broke up she insisted on having primary custody, and got it. She violated the terms in some serious ways, especially when it came to my visitation rights, so that's been reversed, but she's never given up trying to pry him away from me."

"Were she and Eric still in touch?"

"I can't say for sure, but it wouldn't surprise me."

I played another hunch. "Mrs. Danner," I said, "is this your first marriage?"

"It's my second. The first one ended years ago. There were no children. It has no bearing on this case."

"I have to ask you both a personal question. Were you having an affair that broke up your first marriages?"

She said, "Is that question absolutely necessary?"

"I'm afraid so."

I waited. They exchanged a quick, nervous glance, like two people whose past was about to catch up to them.

Paul Danner said, "The answer to your question is yes."

I said, "Only you know how nasty things got, and I'm not asking for the details, but have you calculated for the possibility that the first Mrs. Danner still harbors a grudge and may have got her hooks into Eric and is using him to make it rough on both of you?"

Paul Danner said, "I think that's as good a possibility as any."

Karen Danner got up and returned to the window.

Her husband said, "A few days ago I went to Eric's apartment. I have a key and let myself in. He wasn't there, but some of his stuff was, his computer and stereo and a few items of clothing. It looks like he's gone but plans to return."

"Then why do you think you need me?"

Karen Danner said, "Because if he stays with his mother very long he could return messed up enough to undermine things for us and for the campaign. Excuse me if that sounds mercenary. I honestly want what's best for him."

"Where's his mother?" I said.

Paul Danner said, "I don't know. We haven't spoken for years."

"How old is Eric?"

"He's twenty-one."

"He's a legal adult," I said. "Even if I take the case . . ."

"*If* you take the case," Karen Danner said. She looked startled, as if it hadn't occurred to her that I might not, or that I had a choice.

"You heard me right. *If* I take the case, the best I may be able to do is set up a meeting between you and Eric. I'm not going to kidnap him and deliver him in handcuffs. And I'll need at least twenty-four hours to decide."

Danner said, "Why?"

"To find out some things."

"Find out what that we haven't told you?"

"Things that aren't filtered through the prism of your experience and interests. You came in here with a hunch concerning what's happened to him, but I had to pull it out of you. That leaves me wondering what else I might need to know that you're not telling me."

If there was more, that was his cue to reveal it. Instead, he took a leather-bound checkbook from a breast pocket of his suit jacket and set it on the desk in front of him. I smelled money. He took an expensive looking pen from the same pocket and held his hand over a blank check. Before I could say anything he began filling it out. He signed with a flourish, tore it off and set it on the desk in front of me. It was for $10,000. I let the check lie there lest my touching it be construed as acceptance.

He said, "If you deliver Eric to me, Mr. Pool, that's yours. If you can't manage it but convince me that you've given it your best, it's still yours. If you decide you don't want the job, tear it up and I'll pay you for whatever time you spent in coming to that decision. Here's my card. It has my cell phone and home phone numbers. The campaign has me in town for a couple of days."

He stood, glanced at the check, then at me. He seemed confident that money would buy my assent. Karen Danner was already on her way to the door.

When they had left I put the check in my safe and returned to my desk, put my feet up on it and leaned back in my chair and looked over at my window. The bricks of the wall of the building next door had fallen into shadow.

CHAPTER 2

I called Jill Frye, my *Milwaukee Journal* colleague before it merged with the *Sentinel*. Not long after that merger, and in part because of it, I left my job as an investigative journalist to become a private investigator; Jill stayed on in her position as an investigative journalist and a feature writer.

After my career switch, I retained Jill's services whenever I needed deep research done, a kind of thing for which she has somewhat more talent and patience than I do. We were also, on and off, an item, which is not to say lovers. At the time, we were somewhere between on and off. I wanted, in this case, to tap her encyclopedic knowledge and memory, there being not a public issue or person in Wisconsin on which she wasn't well versed on the background, details, and nuances. She was free, and we agreed to meet at seven o'clock at Delaney's, a restaurant and micro-brewery on Water Street.

I showed up at seven-fifteen, the earliest I could imagine Jill arriving. She came at ten to eight, breezily unapologetic for, and quite possibly unmindful of, being fifty minutes late. Jill, who as far as I know has never missed a deadline, has otherwise no grasp of the reality that time actually passes, that after an hour of talking on the phone or agonizing over wardrobe selections or doing who knows what in the bathroom, she'll be an hour closer to whenever it is she has committed to showing up. I've never told her so, but it's one of the reasons our relationship toggles between on and off and doesn't stay strictly on. She gave me a peck on the cheek and sat across the table from me. A waiter took our orders—a corned beef sandwich and coffee for Jill, fish and chips and house ale for me.

She propped her elbows on the table, rested her chin on her interlaced fingers, and said, "How was the retreat, Barry?"

"Quiet. No talk. And needless to say no computers or radio or TV or cell phones or pagers or . . ."

"For that you went all the way to Kentucky? Sounds uncivilized."

"Just the opposite. And yes, for that I went all the way to Kentucky. Very refreshing, and well worth the trip."

"I half expected you to come back with your head shaved and in a hooded robe."

"The Trappists don't shave their heads," I said. "Also no newspapers, so I'm out of touch. What's happening around town?"

"Plenty, but the biggest thing going down is the Travis Isely case."

"Things were just starting to heat up before I left. Honest opinion—did the cops step over the line on this one and commit murder?"

"I don't do opinion. That's Terrell's department. He's already devoted two columns to saying, not exactly that Travis Isely got what he deserved—nobody *deserves* to get shot seventeen times, as Terrell pointed out—but that he was a thug and a gang-banger and that he died the way he lived. A good part of the first column listed the particulars of Isely's rap sheet, the violence and mayhem he's been committing in the last ten or so years of his short life. It came out on the day of his funeral, the same edition that showed his mother on the front page weeping over the casket. The second column was mostly Terrell defending himself against charges of insensitivity. That's Terrell for you. Truth and honesty at any cost."

"You'd think he'd know better. I trust he's getting what *he* deserves."

"In spades. Excuse the word choice. Traitor to his race, and all that. Threats, even. He's hired Malcolm Oakly to bodyguard for him until things blow over."

"Glad to hear The Oak's getting legitimate work."

"Problem is," she said, "it might not blow over for a while. The MPD put the officers on paid leave pending an internal investigation. Want to know more?"

"By force of habit."

"Of the four officers who fired shots, two were black, one was Hispanic, and one was white. All were male. That part you probably know. According to LeRoy Givens, who's stirring the pot in his usual fashion, the skin color of the ones in uniform isn't what counts; it's that they're all blue, and blue in Milwaukee means the assumption that if you're a young black male, you're armed and dangerous and guilty. Chief Foley has threatened to have WBMR shut down and Givens arrested for incitement to riot."

"Has the chief heard of the Constitution?"

"You wouldn't think so to hear him. It gets better, though. Several big names in the civil rights movement are threatening to converge on Milwaukee if the MPD whitewashes this."

"For instance?"

"Junius Cato. He's considering coming north and camping out at the mosque on North Teutonia, to keep a closer eye on things. Not to be outdone, David Sojourner is going around saying, 'Milwaukee needs vision, not derision'. I haven't talked to anyone who knows what that means, but it's obvious whose vision he thinks Milwaukee needs."

"Big brother Chicago's," I said.

Jill nodded. "Even the Reverend Marcus Starr is taking an interest, and may come all the way from New York. It's hard to tell if these guys are acting in concert, or if each is afraid of being upstaged by the others. And of course the fact that this is an election year raises the stakes. Anyway, a whole lot hangs on that MPD report, which will take who knows how long."

The waiter brought our orders. Jill took a bite of her sandwich, which was cut into triangles, washed it down with black coffee and said, "Your turn. Is it a case?"

"Yes, but I haven't decided if I want it. I'm hoping I'll learn something from you that will help. It concerns Paul Danner's son, who may or may not be missing, or kidnapped, or something."

"May or may not?"

"What I've been told by Danner and his wife is that they haven't heard from him since before the end of Marquette's spring semester, about two weeks ago. He thinks he may have gone to join his mother somewhere, but I had to work to get that out of him. Before I proceed I'd like to know if the kid is running from something or to something, or both. I know you can't answer that for me, but I have a feeling that I can get closer to an answer if I know more about Danner. Not the public person so much as the private stuff regarding his former wife and the current one. When they were in my office today, I got the feeling that there was still more that they weren't saying."

Jill ate some of her sandwich. I got out my pocket notebook and a mechanical pencil and waited.

What followed was Jill at her best—as thorough, nuanced, and organized a presentation as she'd make if I had given her a month to research and plan. She sketched Paul Danner's rise through the political ranks to his current status as the Republican Party's candidate for the U.S. Senate. Some of that I already knew. Most of what followed, between bites of her sandwich, I didn't know.

"His marriage to Karen Danner came about the time of his second run for the state legislature," Jill said. "He had run before and lost, probably for being too far right. When he ran again it was on a much more moderate platform. He won, and after a couple of terms in the house, he moved up to the state Senate. Through all this, he was backed, financially and otherwise, by the well-heeled Republican establishment and by his new wife, who seems to have serious money. In fact, her arrival on the scene and the turnaround in his political fortunes gives rise to a sort of chicken-and-egg question. I don't know much about Karen Danner before she hooked up with him except that she was previously married."

"In my office this afternoon the tension in the air was palpable when the subject of his ex-wife came up. What can you tell me about her?"

"Some. Her name is Frieda. I'm not certain why she and Paul Danner split up, but a couple of things stick in my mind. The timing, for one thing, by which I mean how soon after the split that he began appearing in public with the current Mrs. Danner. Another is the impression I got that Frieda Danner was kind of an alpha female—a controller, a ball buster of an extreme right-wing variety. She's the daughter of Russell Ingram, a neo-Nazi white supremacist and the resident patriarch of a compound somewhere up north, around Rhinelander. It's part church, so-called, part right-wing militia. Testosterone cases who never outgrew the thrill of wearing uniforms and carrying weapons and marching and shouting in unison."

She sipped coffee and continued. "Frieda Danner hurt her husband's prospects in his first run for the state legislature with some pretty shrill stuff that registered with the general public as insensitivity toward the poor and minorities, among others. Depending on who's spinning the story, even downright racism. Not long after Danner lost the election, they broke up. The split was fairly acrimonious, and publicly so, at least for a while. One got the sense that he'd never realize his political ambitions with her as his wife. By most accounts, he bettered his situation when he remarried, certainly politically and financially, and probably in terms of domestic happiness as well. If I had to guess where Frieda Danner ended up, her father's compound is where I'd start. Whether or not she'd still be there is another matter."

"But if she is, and if Eric Danner has gone to her, and if I take the case, then I'd be venturing into Skinhead Nation."

"Mm-hm." She had eaten half her sandwich. She pointed to the remaining half on the plate. "You want the rest of this?"

"No thanks."

Jill said, "It seems to me that if you want a place to start, it might be with this question: When the dust settled between Paul Danner and his first wife, was she left with a desire to hurt him that hasn't faded with time?"

"And if so, what better way than through his son? I suggested that possibility to him this morning. He didn't dismiss it."

"While he's running for the United States Senate."

"Double whammy."

"Do you think you'll take the case?"

"I still don't know," I said. "Eric Danner's twenty-one, and I don't rescue adults who don't want to be rescued. Nor am I thrilled about the prospect of taking on the neo-Nazis. Part of me, too, wants to stick around town to see how this Travis Isely case unfolds."

I had finished my fish and chips and beer. Jill didn't want to take the remaining half of her sandwich home and couldn't persuade me to do so. I paid and we left.

I walked her down the street to her car. Before getting in she leaned back against the driver's side door, very much the temptress, and said, "I've got more for you, but I can only reveal it at my place or yours."

Knowing Jill, I had prepared myself for the moment. I leaned forward at the waist, not to grind against her, and gave her a light, brief kiss.

"What you gave me inside is enough to go on for now," I said.

She pouted. "Why don't you just go ahead and take vows?"

"That day may come. In the meantime I don't want to carry fornication into the confessional."

"Then *don't*."

"We've been over this before," I said.

"*Ad infinitum.*"

She got in and drove off, her squealing tires accusing me of prudery. I went to my car and headed for my house on the East Side.

I went in to find my answering machine message light blinking. It was from Paul Danner. He needed to see me again. He said unless he heard from me otherwise he'd come to my office the next morning around ten o'clock.

I didn't much like his assuming that he could summon me to work on a Saturday morning, and entertained the idea of not getting back to him and not showing up, thereby sending the message that I wasn't interested. On the other side of the scale was that $10,000 check in my safe in my office and how much I needed the money.

Then it occurred to me that I now had a criterion for deciding whether or not to take the case: I had learned from Jill more about his ex-wife than he had revealed earlier that day. I'd meet him, and if he was still coy about her and seemed to be trying to lure me in without full disclosure, I'd turn him down flat. If he was forthcoming, then I'd consider it. But even then I'd have to think hard about how much I wanted to take on the risk that the case might entail.

CHAPTER 3

I arrived at my office on Oakland Avenue a little before ten and made a pot of coffee. Within a few minutes a knock came at the door. I went and opened it.

Paul Danner stood in the hall alone. He looked like a kid playing hooky from school. I invited him in.

I said, "Have a seat. Coffee?"

"I'd love some."

He sat in the chair he had been in the day before. I filled a couple of mugs, set his in front of him then went around the desk with mine and sat. Since he had proposed the meeting, I waited for him to speak. But he seemed to be waiting for me, so I began by stating the obvious.

"You're here alone."

"It was a mistake to come with Karen yesterday," he said. "I couldn't speak as freely as I wanted to. Not that I have secrets to keep from her. It's just that certain stuff regarding my first wife is painful for her—for both of us—and I didn't want to drag them out in front of her all over again."

"Does she know you're here now?"

He looked over at my window, where she had stood the day before.

"No, but she won't mind as long as it helps," he said.

"Helps."

"Works. Smoothes things over. Makes the trouble go away quickly and quietly so that we can get on with our lives and the campaign. If that means Eric's returning to us, that will be fine with Karen, as long as he doesn't muck things up. But we're getting ahead of ourselves. Have you decided to take the case?"

"No," I said. "What you tell me this morning, or don't tell me, will likely make the difference. But I want the whole truth, as you see it, and nothing but. You're going to have to drag out the things you didn't want to yesterday in front of your wife, even if you think doing so could scare me off. It's a chance you have to take if you want me on the job."

He lifted his mug and looked down at his coffee as if for some clue how to start. He drank some. Then, in what struck me as a bit of histrionics, he pulled down the corners of his mouth, set his jaw purposefully, and started in.

"Frieda and I split up in part because of my affair with Karen. There was more to it, though. Much more. The big issue between me and Frieda was ideology. We were both pretty far right when it came to politics. I was a lawyer with a successful practice in criminal law, a prosecutor. Some people I associated with professionally urged me to run for Waukesha County States Attorney, so I did, but in doing so, I had to tone down some of the more extreme things Frieda and I believed in. She went along with that, although grudgingly."

"What were some of these extreme views?"

"Before I tell you, I want to say that Frieda was always much more militant about this stuff than I was. Her father was and still is a hard-core white supremacist, and she turned out to be more her father's daughter than I realized when I married her."

"It's hard to imagine your marrying her without knowing where she stood," I said.

He seemed annoyed at that observation, but I couldn't tell if it was at me for saying it or at his having to face the truth about himself.

He said, "Back to your question. The issues were immigration, crime, homosexuality, affirmative action, to name a few. Frieda went along with my having to tone down the rhetoric in my run for States Attorney because she saw it as a means to an end, the end being to get me into a position from which I could have more power to advance her—our—social and political agenda. What she didn't count on was that I would gradually turn into the thing I was pretending to be. Mind you, I'd still be thought pretty conservative on most of these issues, but I had moderated. And it seemed the more I did, the more shrill and obsessive Frieda became. We managed to stay together, though, somehow. Then after I ran for the state legislature and lost, I could see that I was going to have to move even more toward the center if I wanted to advance politically."

"Did you want to?"

"I *did* want to," he said. "By that time I had the bit in my mouth, and I was being encouraged to run again. It was around then that Karen and I were becoming . . . *entwined*. She and her husband were among those backing me. They had money, lots of it, most of it hers. One thing led to another, and we ended up in a relationship. How that happened isn't pertinent here, but I'm afraid we didn't do a very good job of hiding it.

"In the meantime, Frieda was moving even further to the right, maybe as a reaction to my new thinking and positions. She acted at times like I was a threat to everything she believed in, and I came to see her as a threat to everything I'd worked for." The memory unsettled his face. "She accused me of making a devil's bargain with gay rights and diversity, among other issues. By the time the split became final she seemed more obsessed with my politics than with my infidelity, which by then she had caught wind of. She called me a weakling and accused me of having sold out to godless mongrel scum. She actually used language like that. Two years after that first loss, by which time Karen and I were married, I ran again and won. Four years after that I was in the state Senate and even closer to the political center."

He winced before continuing. "But I hadn't heard the last of Frieda. She called and wrote me letters full of threats and accusations, although she was careful to stop short of anything that could land her in legal trouble. By then she had gone north to join her father, and I wanted to believe she was too far removed geographically to do any harm. But sometimes she'd call and Karen would answer and catch the brunt of it. Karen swears she's a paranoid-schizophrenic, and I think she may be right."

"What of Eric in all this?" By this time I was beginning to feel like a shrink.

He winced again.

"I'm afraid he got caught in the middle. I'm not going to lay all his troubles on Frieda; God knows I could have been a better father. But even before we broke up, Frieda was always trying to use him to manipulate me, but at the same time withholding affection from him. From a young age he struggled, mentally and psychologically. He was in and out of various kinds of therapy, on and off drugs meant to even out his behavior and moods, all with mixed results.

"When Frieda and I divorced, Eric was fourteen and she was awarded custody. But she did a number of things that violated the agreement. She took him north to her father's compound, which was technically not against the rules, but in doing so she made him unavailable when he was supposed to be visiting me. This went on for a while, until a judge gave custody of Eric to me."

I said, "I didn't bring this up yesterday with your wife here, but he sounds like a candidate for suicide. Has it occurred to you that the car accidents you mentioned were attempts to take his own life?"

"It *has* occurred to me. One therapist we took him to suggested the same thing, but I've been resisting the idea."

"Do you think he's gone to be with his mother?"

"It's the only thing I can come up with," he said. "I have no trouble believing that she hasn't forgotten her vow to take me down. And, with me running for the Senate, what better time? My feeling is that she reestablished contact with Eric somehow and is using him to try to make my life miserable. If she caught wind of his getting mugged and robbed by some black guys, she might have tried to use that as leverage. I also think it's possible that his going to her may be an attempt on his part to win her affection. If she's with her father, then she's on a compound near a small tourist town up north called Deering. They have some acreage on a lake with a lodge. It's where she took Eric a few times."

"Since we talked yesterday," I said, "I've learned some things about the place. I have to say, I'm not thrilled about the prospect of walking by myself into Skinhead Nation to get your son, who may be there of his own free will."

"Take my word for it, he's not, even if he thinks he is. Anyway, I don't blame you. When I wrote that check yesterday, I was trying to provide an incentive to overcome any misgivings you might have."

"And you did. But I don't know if I can let money trump risk in this case. Have you told me everything?"

"Almost. There's one thing more. Before Karen and I married, she was Karen Pierce. Her name before that, her maiden name, was Nussbaum."

"She's Jewish."

"Half, from her dad's side."

"Does your ex-wife know that?"

"Yes. She went absolutely ballistic when she found out."

I sat and thought. About the potential danger involved if I took the case. About that $10,000 check in my safe only a few feet away and how badly I needed an infusion of cash and the things I could do with it, like getting the brakes on my car fixed and paying a large plumbing bill that was overdue, maybe even buying a Bucks season ticket. Paul Danner watched me sit and think. I looked over at my window. The bricks were dull gray.

Danner said, "Maybe we should take this one step at a time."

He reached into a pants pocket and pulled out a key that was attached by a metal ring to a brass rectangle. He set it on my desk and pushed it toward me.

"This is the key to Eric's place near Marquette. It's an apartment building in the 1000 block of North 18th Street called Aspen Court. Karen's family owns the building. We've been paying Eric's rent and I keep a key. When I went there to check things out, I detected evidence that someone else had been there."

"What kind of evidence?"

"In the second bedroom, there was an ashtray full of cigarette butts. Eric's not a smoker, at least as far as I know. As I said, some of Eric's clothes and his computer are still there. His SUV seems to be gone; I looked all around for it. It's a red Ford Explorer." He gave me the license number, and I wrote it down. "I'd feel better if a trained investigator gave the place a once-over. I'll pay you just to do that, then if you don't want to go further, I won't force you to."

I didn't bother pointing out that, strictly speaking, I wasn't a trained investigator in the sense that he meant, or that in saying he wouldn't force me to take the case he was suggesting that he could if he wanted to, and had thus spoken nonsense.

"Perhaps if you went there you might find something I overlooked," he said.

And perhaps he was calculating that if I took one step I'd find it easier to go forward than to go back.

I picked up the key from my desk. "I'll go on Monday."

"I appreciate this."

"You shouldn't. I'm not committed to anything."

CHAPTER 4

On Monday morning I drove to Aspen Court Apartments on North 18th Street. It was a leafy residential neighborhood with a mix of big and small old houses and a couple of other apartment buildings. I parked on the street.

I had arranged to meet Mike Tiggs there, a freelance techie that I hired whenever I needed computer work done. Aspen Court consisted of four apartments on each of three levels, with galleries facing the street that gave access to the outside entrances. A lot of the cars parked on the street and in the small attached lot had Marquette parking permits in the front windshield. I went up to the middle story and let myself into Eric Danner's apartment.

Near where I stood inside the entrance a couch and some soft chairs were arranged around a cart with a television and accessory equipment. A coffee table between the TV and the couch held a few magazines and newspapers. Beyond that area, next to a wall on the left, was a desk with a computer and a printer. A small dining table sat up against a waist-high partition. I walked through to the kitchen.

Magnets held slips of paper to the front of the refrigerator. I looked at all of them but found only one thing of interest—a small sheet with handwriting that said "Moms cell" above a number. I copied the number into my pocket notebook. On top of the fridge were an opened Cheerios box and a half-full bag of potato chips held closed with a plastic spring clip. The inside had some moldy cheese and cold cuts, and an inch of rancid milk in a half-gallon jug. A hall led from the kitchen to a bathroom, two bedrooms and a utility closet.

Mike Tiggs knocked at the front door. I let him in and showed him the computer.

"I'm interested in knowing the contents of this," I said. "But I have no password or username, nothing to gain access. Is that a problem?"

Tiggs smiled the smile that those with his skills and knowledge reserve for the likes of me. He sat down to work, and I looked around some more.

The first of the two bedrooms was relatively neat. The bed was more or less made, and a couple of shirts and a pair of pants hung in the closet. Bureau drawers held a t-shirt and some socks. I looked in, under, and behind everything and found nothing of interest.

The other bedroom was a different story. The bed was unmade, and a large ashtray was about two-thirds full of cigarette butts. No clothes or other personal items were in the closet or the dresser drawers. I searched the room the same way I had searched the other one, with the same result.

I went back out to the living room and picked up the phone receiver and heard a dial tone. I used a remote control and turned on the TV; a satellite channel appeared on the screen. I turned it off.

Tiggs was still at work. "Your boy was into some spooky stuff, although I've seen worse," he said.

I spent some time searching the other rooms as I had the bedrooms then sat on the sofa and sifted through the reading matter on the coffee table—a *Sports Illustrated*, a three-week-old copy of the *Journal Sentinel*, some slick soft-core porn disguised as a men's health magazine with a mailing label on it. The name was Brad Schale at what appeared to be a rural address near Deering, Wisconsin. I copied the address into my pocket notebook. I thumbed through the magazines while Tiggs worked. It took him a little over an hour.

"I'm done," Tiggs said. I pulled up a chair next to where he sat at the computer.

"I checked websites visited and emails sent and received," he said. "I sifted out the obvious spam and made hard copies of the rest, the emails in full and home pages of some of the websites, enough to give you a feel for the guy and his interests."

He indicated some papers that he had placed on the dining table. "A lot of the emails, especially the more recent ones, are to and from someone named Frieda Schale. I did some tracking while I was online, and she appears to be near a small town called Deering, north of Rhinelander. I printed out her address and cell phone number."

He pulled a sheet of paper from the top of the pile and showed me. The address matched the one I had just copied from the magazine. The phone number matched the one on the front of the refrigerator.

"You can sift through it," Mike said, "but by way of summary, about half the websites are porn. Most of the rest are white supremacist sites, including a neo-Nazi, skinhead outfit called North Star. It happens to be located near Deering. Charming bunch. Out to rid the world of the Jewish-Negro conspiracy to dilute the white race. And they aren't squeamish about how to go about it. Even if I was white I'd be spooked by these guys."

"Any chance I can have the user name and password Eric Danner used to get online and to email?"

That smile again. He nodded toward the printouts. "It's in the pile."

"Thanks, Mike. Send me a bill."

"You can believe I will."

Tiggs left. I sat at the dining table in front of the stack of pages he had printed. I got out a pen and highlighter and started in.

The emails were organized so that exchanges on the same subject were together in chronological order: message-reply, reply-to-reply, and so on.

The earliest was one sent to Eric Danner from Frieda Schale. I assumed she was Paul Danner's first wife, and wondered if he was aware of her new last name. It was from the previous November, before Thanksgiving, and was brief, consisting mostly of greetings and good wishes and ending with an off-handed invitation to Eric to "come north for a visit" whenever he was free. It seemed that they hadn't been in touch for a while and that she had learned from someone other than his father that he was enrolled at Marquette. Another from her conveyed holiday greetings just before Christmas. His first reply wasn't until January and didn't mention the Thanksgiving invitation, or the car wreck he had been in.

All the correspondence between then and mid-March was

one way, from her to him, and, again, consisted of a mix of pleasantries and invitations to him to join her for a weekend getaway, or for spring break. The invitations sounded less off-handed as they progressed. His few responses were perfunctory and didn't acknowledge her invitations.

Then came a turn.

An email from him to her recounted his being mugged and robbed at night as he was walking along Wisconsin Avenue on his way home from campus. He identified the attackers only as "some black guys." She replied with sympathy and a request for more details. He replied that he had also been taunted with racial slurs and mockery of his manhood, that they were threatening to cut him when two cops came along in a squad car, but not soon enough to catch the guys. He made note of the fact that one cop was black, the other Hispanic. The cops called an ambulance, which took him to an emergency room, where he was stitched up and bandaged by "more blacks." He said he tried to reach his father to let him know what happened, but couldn't get past his staff, who were screening his calls.

His mother replied, again expressing sympathy and the wish that they were closer—it was unclear if by that term she referred to geography—so that she could be of more help. She exhorted him to remember the things she had tried to teach him since he was young, without specifying what those things were, and again encouraged him to "come north to be with [his] own kind."

His response to that invitation smacked of approach-avoidance. After another entreaty from her, he sounded somewhat more inclined to go north to join her, but said he wasn't free to get away because of school. She replied that she might send "Brad" down to help him sort out his priorities and even act as bodyguard and to escort him north if he decided to come. Eric replied noncommittally. Her next reply was more insistence than suggestion. His next message, three days later, referred to Brad's presence on the scene, with about equal parts skepticism about how it would work out and resignation that he guessed it would have to. The picture that emerged was of a Brad that had bullied his way into Eric's apartment and life and threatened to become The Thing That Wouldn't Leave.

I went to the computer and got onto North Star's website. It contained a mix of text and photos of scenes from the North Star compound. In one, Russell Ingram declaimed to a roomful of followers from behind a lectern. On both sides of him, flags on poles hung limp, their symbols obscured, but I could see enough to know that neither of them was Old Glory.

The written stuff was apologetics, position statements, "facts" and historical background. I read some parts and skimmed others. There were a couple of ominous references to "The Gathering," which sounded imminent. Taken all together, the stuff I saw and read tended to confirm my theory about the connection between evil and stupidity. Brad Schale's name didn't appear anywhere, but the name Max Schale did. He seemed to be Russell Ingram's first lieutenant and heir apparent as leader of North Star. The menu bar on the left included links to websites of like-minded groups. I clicked on some and browsed a while then went to the phone.

I first called information and asked for phone numbers for Russell Ingram, Brad Schale, and Max Schale. Brad Schale wasn't listed. Ingram and Max Schale had the same number.

I called. A man picked up on the fifth ring.

"Hello."

"Can I speak with Eric Danner?"

The line went dead.

I went back to the computer and browsed some more of the links from North Star's website. After about ten minutes I called again.

"Hello." The voice sounded different, older and huskier.

"Is Eric Danner around?"

"Who wants to know?"

Progress. "I'd like to talk to him."

"You didn't answer my question."

"That makes us even," I said.

The line went dead.

I called "Moms cell."

The third ring got an answer—what I think was "Hello," from what I guessed to be a female, middle-aged or older. She sounded out of breath and flustered. I tried a different tack.

"Can you get a message to Eric for me? I'm a friend from Marquette, and I'm trying to get in touch with him to pay back the money I borrowed from him before he took off."

She fumbled for words for a moment then said, "How did you get this number? How did you know Eric was . . ." She drew in a sharp breath, then with raised voice and in a demanding tone said, "Who is this, and what are you doing calling from Eric's apartment?" I hadn't calculated for caller ID on her end.

I hung up. Using only the phone, I was fairly certain that I had learned what I needed to know—that Eric Danner was on the North Star compound in Wisconsin's far north woods. Barry Pool, ace detective. I went back to the computer and shut down and left with the stack of papers that Mike Tiggs had printed out.

CHAPTER 5

As I was closing the door behind me a young female with a book bag slung over one shoulder came up the stairs and went to the door of the apartment next to Eric's. She pulled some keys from a pocket of her shorts and selected one, all the while watching me out of the corner of one eye. Feminine caution. I kept my distance.

"Excuse me," I said. I stood with my hands behind my back in non-attack mode. Key in the lock, hand on the key, she turned her head but not her body. She had curly auburn hair to her shoulders and a sweet, pretty face with a peaches-and-cream complexion.

"I'm looking for Eric Danner," I said. "I wonder if you know him."

"I *knew* him," she said, poised to open her door and escape inside.

I said, "I'm trying to locate him for his father. Do you have any idea where he might be?"

"I'm afraid not," she said. "I haven't seen Eric since before the end of school."

I got a business card out of my wallet, took one step toward her, leaned forward and held it out. She took it and read it and looked at me.

"A private eye. Is Eric in trouble?"

"That's what I'm trying to find out. Eric's father also hasn't heard from him since before school ended, and he's concerned."

"I used to see him about every day." She had relaxed some. "For a while there we were riding to campus together. We had classes in the same building, and our schedules were close, so we took turns driving."

She looked again at the card and said, "This goes against all my training, Mr. Pool, but I guess you're safe. You can come in and talk if you want. My name's Nancy Kane."

We went in. The layout of her place was a mirror image of Eric's. We sat at her dining table. I declined her offer of a glass of apple juice.

I said, "Did you and Eric talk much? Did you know him well enough to guess where he might be?"

She tick-tocked her head. "We talked some, mostly about school. He was undecided as far as a major goes. He was undecided about a lot of things. At times he seemed like a lost soul. He also had girlfriend problems, but lots of guys I know do. The straight ones, anyway. I felt sorry for him. I wanted to help, but he was kind of beyond my reach."

"Why did you want to help?"

She looked at me and thought a moment. She seemed to be trying to assess my level of understanding so that she could fashion an appropriate answer.

"Call it a spiritual imperative," she said. "Eric seemed to be muddling through, but then he got mugged, and things went downhill from there. He got less and less interested in school. He didn't go out much, at least that I could see. Then that creep moved in with him."

"Was the creep's name Brad?"

"Yes. I shouldn't call people names like that, but he was scary."

"Scary in what way?"

"Crude, aggressive, full of himself. And he had this ugly sneer that never went away." She cringed. "He looked like somebody that has contempt for everything."

"Did you see much of Brad?"

"Not a lot. Just knowing he was around was spooky enough. He drove Eric's SUV. Sometimes he had friends over, even when Eric wasn't around. That was the scariest part. They drank and were loud. I don't think Eric had much choice in the matter. A couple of times I spent the night with a friend until they went away."

"Can you describe Brad for me?"

"He had short, dirty-blond hair and blue eyes. He was maybe five-ten with big muscles, but not the attractive kind. They were just lumpy. He wore skimpy, sleeveless t-shirts, or none at all. Once or twice he stood out on the balcony smoking without a shirt on. It was gross. Sometimes he looked like he was high. And he had tattoos—a skull, crossed daggers dripping blood, double lightning bolts or something on the back of one hand."

"Are you sure they were lightning bolts?"

"What do you mean?"

I got out my pocket notebook, opened it to a blank page and

drew two jagged parallel lines. I held the sheet for her to see.

"Yeah, like that," she said. "Are you saying those aren't lightning bolts?"

"They can be, but they're also the symbol of the Nazi SS."

She gaped at me in retroactive fear.

"Do you know who any of Eric's teachers were?" I said.

"He had Dr. Jacobs for freshman English in the spring," she said. "I had him last year, and Eric and I talked about him some. We both liked him."

"Will you be around all summer?"

"Yes. I'm taking classes and working. Why?"

"Eric might come back. It's hard to say when, but if he does, with or without the other guy, will you call me? You have my card."

"If you think it'll help Eric, I will."

"It might."

I left and went to my car and drove home. On the way I wondered how I should feel about an attractive young female being so sure I was safe.

CHAPTER 6

Marquette's website indicated that Dr. Jacobs was teaching a short story class during the summer session, which had just started. On Tuesday morning I called his office phone and left a message on his answering machine. A couple of hours later he called back. I gave him a sketchy outline of the case, naming Eric Danner. He agreed to meet me that afternoon in his office.

Jacobs was on the third floor of Coughlin Hall. His door was open, and when I appeared in it he stood. We shook hands over his desk and introduced ourselves. He was a middle-aged white guy with glasses and thinning hair, a mustache and a goatee. He had on khaki pants with cuffs, a blue denim shirt with a knit tie loose at the collar—the uniform of the liberal arts academic. He told me to call him Bill and invited me to sit.

"I used to read your stuff in the *Journal,*" he said. "I wondered what happened to you."

"The merger happened."

"You got cut?"

"No. Without competition the edge was gone. When they asked me to do feel-good features for the Leisure Section I knew it was time to move on."

"And here you are," he said.

"Here I am. By the way, I got your name from Nancy Kane. She lives in an apartment next to Eric Danner's and knew he had taken you for a class."

Jacobs's smile revealed a hint of the satyr. "Charming girl, Nancy."

"Yes."

I laid out the case for him in more detail than I had given him over the phone.

"I realize there may be teacher-student confidentiality issues involved here," I said, "but I'm wondering if you saw something in Eric or remember anything that might help me get a handle on him."

"Eric was a below-average student," Jacobs said. "Not a skilled writer or a clear thinker, and with no apparent motivation to become either one, at least from what I could see. At the rate he was going, I suppose he might have eked out a C in my course, but then he more or less quit coming. This was sometime in March. He missed an entire week, then returned for one more class, but from then on he was finished with the semester for all intents and purposes."

"And you failed him."

He looked at me intently and said, "He failed himself. It's a distinction I insist on. But concerning clues to his character, a couple of things were telling. For various purposes, I divide the class into small groups. They discuss issues, review each other's papers, make joint presentations. Eric didn't take well to that kind of work. He was standoffish and uncomfortable and didn't contribute much. I thought he may have felt like he was in over his head. He was with some very sharp kids—bright, ambitious and motivated. One was an African American female; another was a Jewish kid from New York. After a while, though, I got the sense that he didn't like working with minorities."

"What gave you that sense?"

"His journal and some things he said in class. Their journals are a place where they can express themselves freely without concern for grammar and the other things that they have to be mindful of in graded writing. They're supposed to write three entries every week. The theory is that it helps them find their voices as writers. Before Eric went missing his entries were perfunctory and invariably negative—complaints about political correctness, affirmative action, crime and the criminal justice system. And it was the same with the few times he spoke up in class. Our discussions are pretty wide-ranging. Sometimes we get into politics and social issues. The thing is, on some issues—hyper political correctness, for instance—I tended to be on his side. But in an academic setting there are right ways and wrong ways to argue. Eric's were invariably wrong. I suppose I was slow on the draw, but I finally realized that he was putting a racial twist to everything.

"When he came back after being gone for a week, he turned in his journal. He had made up the entries he missed. They were full of rage over being mugged and robbed, and over who had done the mugging and robbing, to the point of being overtly racist."

"After he disappeared for good, did you try to get in touch

with him?"

"No. Rightly or wrongly, I don't chase after students who go AWOL. That doesn't happen much here at Marquette, but when it does I prefer to treat them like adults and let them learn that acts have consequences. I admit that may be a rationalization for the fact that as I've gotten older I've grown more particular about how I spend my time and energy."

"Did he ever write about his biological mother? Her name is Frieda."

"Not that I can remember."

I thought for a moment and couldn't come up with anything else to ask. I stood to leave.

"I still have Eric's journal," Jacobs said.

I sat again. "And?"

"And if you think it might help, you can have it. It's revealing in certain ways that I've mentioned, but I can't remember anything that would serve as a clue to his whereabouts. You might pick up on something I missed or can't remember."

He got up and took a spiral notebook from a shelf and handed it to me.

"Are you sure this is ethical?" I said.

"I'm sure it isn't. Maybe it's my way of trying to help. Or maybe I'm trying to assuage my conscience for not taking action when someone like Eric goes off the rails."

As I got up to leave I noticed that his window looked out over a grassy expanse, crisscrossed with walkways, at the other end of which was the St. Joan of Arc Chapel. Jacobs joined his line of sight to mine.

He said, "The post-modernists look at that and see irony."

"You have post-modernists at Marquette?"

"They're everywhere."

"What do you see?" I said.

He smiled. "An antidote for post-modernism."

I left with Eric Danner's journal.

CHAPTER 7

I took the journal to my office. Instead of making coffee, I got a bottle of Bass Pale Ale out of my mini-fridge, poured it into a glass, sat at my desk and opened the notebook.

Before starting to read I flipped through the pages for a quick visual impression. The entries were written in black ballpoint. I've never put much stock in the claims of graphologists to be able to infer character from handwriting, but I could see a marked difference in the penmanship between the early entries and the later ones, and I couldn't help but think that that signified something.

The most legible entries, the early ones, were in a plain, plodding script; some dealt with mundane matters—the price of textbooks, the price of gas, complaints about having to keep a journal. Bill Jacobs had said that the students were to use their journals to find their voices as writers. At least in those first entries, Eric Danner hadn't found his, or if he had, it wasn't a very interesting or distinctive one; the language and tone were stiff, with lots of passive voice, overreaching on vocabulary, diffidence, and self-consciousness.

He seemed to gain more fluency, and express more frustration, in entries on relationships—with women, with his parents, with friends (what few he seemed to have)—and on the political and social issues Jacobs had mentioned.

The entries he had written after being mugged appeared to have been scratched in haste or in anger or both, sometimes almost to the point of being indecipherable. He castigated himself for his weakness and wrote of a desire to strengthen and arm himself, even to build alliances, so that that kind of thing could never happen again. He also wrote of a desire for revenge.

On my second bottle of ale, I realized that a verbal picture had emerged from the pages of Eric's journal that matched the photo of him that Paul Danner had given me—of someone lost and looking for answers, for an identity, for something larger than himself to latch onto and call meaningful, or at least to call his; of someone fearful that he would never find those things.

Nothing solid emerged in the way of a clue or a lead I could use to confirm my suspicion that he was on the North Star compound.

When I finished I put the notebook in my safe. Before closing the door, I pulled out Paul Danner's $10,000 check and looked at it. I counted the zeros. I put it back, returned to my desk and looked over at my window.

I felt roughly equidistant between Bill Jacobs's hands-off stance and Nancy Kane's "spiritual imperative" to help, neither hooked on the case nor ready to turn my back on it.

I swirled, then drained, the last drops of ale in the glass. I studied the brick wall outside my window. It was neither bright nor dim. I was certain of only two things. One was that, in my meager economy, ten-thousand dollars was a lot of money. The other was that going it alone against a gang of neo-Nazi skinhead thugs, on their ground, was a lot of risk. What I didn't know, and didn't know how I'd come to know, was which would trump the other.

CHAPTER 8

When I awoke the next morning around seven A.M., I couldn't recall deciding to sleep overnight on the couch in my office. Neither could I recall opening and drinking a third bottle of ale. But I must have done both, for there I was, still in my clothes, that third bottle of ale empty on the table nearby. I also couldn't recall deciding to take the Danner case, but I awoke with the unsettling certainty that I would.

Had it been more of a conscious decision, I might have commended myself, as I'm not by nature brave or intrepid or a risk-taker, but it wasn't. I was simply certain that that was what I'd do, more certain that I would go north in search of Eric Danner than that I would return undamaged, or that I would return at all. I suppose the deciding factor was the number of zeros on Paul Danner's check. Maybe too the risk appealed to me. Up to then in my career as a private investigator,

I still hadn't faced any real danger, much less fired a shot, and I felt untested.

I had once done a feature for the *Journal* on Milwaukee PIs. To a person, they all spoke of how their work bore no resemblance to the life of fictional detectives. They said it was mostly mundane, tedious, even boring, involving lots of waiting and watching and digging among records. Every one of them owned one or more guns; none of them had ever fired a shot except on the practice range. So when I made the career switch from investigative journalism to private investigations, I had no illusions about the kind of work I was getting into. I figured I'd be working almost exclusively for husbands and wives who suspected their spouses of infidelity. And, except for a handful of cases involving fraud and employee theft, that expectation proved to be on target. (One husband I had exposed as a gigolo threatened revenge, but nothing ever came of it.)

Still, I thought I should prepare as best I could for whatever came my way. I started by working on strength and conditioning at the YMCA. I ran the track and spent time in the weight room. I considered martial arts training but discarded the idea, figuring it would take too long to become proficient. I ruled out boxing for more or less the same reason. I hadn't thrown a punch since fifth grade when I got in a schoolyard scrap with Joey Stallworth. The fight was a draw because a teacher broke it up before either of us could do any damage.

And there was the question of weaponry. I knew almost nothing about guns, so I did some research and asked the advice of a cop friend, who recommended a gun shop in West Allis that sold new and used guns and had a firing range. I went there and was lucky to get a clerk who was patient and didn't condescend to me.

I ended up with a five-shot Charter Arms Undercover .38 special with a two-inch barrel, and a Browning Vest Pocket with two six-shot clips. The Browning was World War II vintage, a virtual antique but not priced like one, in good working order, and at four and at half inches overall length and only thirteen ounces, I could carry it and the extra clip unobtrusively in a baggy side pocket of a pair of cargo pants or a sport coat. Together they set me back just under $500.

Part of the deal was a certain number of hours on the firing range at a discounted rate. I spent time there, and, later, at a range on the south side of Milwaukee, and discovered to my mild surprise and enjoyment that I had a knack for shooting. I could go from empty-handed to a well-placed shot in just under two seconds. At fifteen yards with the .38, I could make a nice tight cluster in the head or chest. Not bad for a scribbler. I took such pleasure in it that I found the purchase worthwhile on that account alone.

None of my preparation, however, meant that I felt equipped to take on northern Wisconsin's violent white supremacist fringe, but there I was, committed to doing so.

I freshened up in my office and made a pot of coffee. At nine o'clock I went to my bank, where I deposited most of the $10,000 check from Paul Danner into my checking account, keeping out $500 in cash and $1,000 in travelers' checks.

I caught a city bus to the nearest car rental business and rented a four-wheel drive Jeep Cherokee for the trip. I drove it back to my house and loaded it with what I thought I might need for a couple of weeks—clothes, accessories, camera, binoculars, tape recorder, guns.

I called Jill at the *Journal Sentinel* to let her know what I was up to. She was away from her desk, so I left a message with the receptionist. I called Paul Danner. Whoever answered for him said he couldn't come to the phone. Not knowing how much his staff people knew, and wanting to be discrete, I said, "Please tell him Barry Pool called and that I'm on my way north. He'll understand."

I locked up and left, not knowing when I'd return, not certain that I would. I drove north out of Milwaukee on Interstate 43. In all this, I acted decisively and without second thoughts or delay, lest they be fatal to my resolve.

CHAPTER 9

I had been to northern Wisconsin and the Upper Peninsula of Michigan a number of times, but this was my first trip to the north in over ten years, and I wasn't looking forward to it.

My first time up there was as a Boy Scout on a camping trip to Porcupine Mountains State Park in the U.P. Years later some college friends and I rented a cabin by a lake in Nicolet National Forest. We canoed and swam and fished and hiked and drank entirely too much beer and made entirely too much drunken noise. Later I did a journalism piece that took me north, a story on a conflict between loggers and Indian tribes that was on the brink of violence. And I once spent some solitary time there on vacation.

I started out enjoying it up north, or thinking I did. The lakes were clear and refreshing, the woods cool and enchanting. But the more I slapped mosquitoes or rubbed noxious repellents on all my exposed surfaces so I wouldn't have to slap mosquitoes, and the more I could see that a fair number of the people who went there to live did so from what struck me as a misanthropic desire to escape the complexities of life elsewhere, the closer I came to realizing that I didn't enjoy being in the north woods after all. I came to suspect, in fact, that I had never liked it as much as I thought. I think I must have got caught up in a kind of group mentality about what a boy, and later a young man, is supposed to feel about spending time in such an environment. In fact, about the only good memory of my time up there was of hearing the loons.

I took I-43 up to Green Bay, where I got on Wisconsin 29 and headed west. At Wausau I stopped for a late lunch then picked up U.S. 51 north, into the deep woods.

The four lanes of 51 and I-39 coincide south to north through the middle of Wisconsin, but not all the way. About three-quarters of the way up, where the towns are smaller and farther apart, the interstate ends and 51 narrows to two lanes. Looking at a map of the area, with its large patches of green indicating the state and national forests and its hundreds of blue patches for the lakes, you can almost smell the pines.

I must apologize to those who would like a detailed naturalist's account of my drive north. I know a deer and a squirrel when I see one and can pretty much distinguish between evergreens and deciduous trees, and, among the latter, a maple from an oak, but that's about the extent of my naturalistic knowledge. For as long as I can remember, the only species I've found worthy of close-up study is *homo sapiens*—his motives and desires and the yearnings of his heart and other organs, or hers, and how those play out on big and small stages. I suppose some of the trees were the lofty balsams of the old Hamm's beer commercials, but about the most I can say along those lines about my drive north is, "Jeepers, it was real pretty."

I got to Minocqua around six o'clock and checked into a motel on a commercial strip. I was no more than half an hour from Deering, my destination and what I assumed would be base camp for my search for Eric Danner, but I wanted plenty of time in Deering to scout for long-term accommodations. I had breakfast the next morning in Minocqua and got into Deering before ten o'clock.

The population sign on the edge of town read 1800, but it looked bigger, no doubt because of the year-round influx of vacationers. Deering's website, which I had looked at before leaving Milwaukee, promoted the town as the place for family fun in every season—fishing, hunting, skiing, snowmobiling. It contained no mention of the presence of white supremacists, no one in the background of the photos giving the Nazi salute.

I drove slowly down the main street, doing reconnaissance. I hadn't yet decided if I wanted to stay in town or out in the countryside. There were lots of places, big and small, for overnight accommodations, and the almost empty parking lots suggested that there would be plenty of vacancies.

I headed out of town and drove the state and county roads, still scouting. Every couple of miles there was a motel next to the road, most of them variations on the same arrangement: rooms in a continuous strip and detached cabins. Some had their own bar and eatery; others were handy to one close by. I stopped at a couple of places to ask about availability and rates. Peak season wouldn't kick in until around the Fourth of July, so I could have a room or a cabin for about $65 a night. At a place called the Whispering Pines, the individual cabins were arrayed behind the main strip of rooms, out of sight of passing traffic on the road. That appealed to me.

"Any chance I can have a cabin for a week?" I said to the proprietor, a guy in his upper years named Vern.

"Yep. I'm already booked starting around July Fourth. Till then you can stay as long as you like."

Vern was a garrulous old gent who very much wanted me to know, among other things, that he had bought The Whispering Pines a few years back for something to do in his retirement. I paid a week's rent in advance for a cabin. It was small and neat, with two beds, a TV and a telephone, and cheap art on the walls that depicted north country nature scenes.

After unpacking I tried calling Nancy Kane on my cell phone to let her know where to reach me in case Eric Danner returned to his apartment while I was up there. It seemed I was out of my coverage area, so I used the room phone. She didn't answer, and I left a message. I called to let Paul Danner know of my whereabouts, too; instead of Danner I got a member of his staff, who said he'd relay my message to the candidate.

I drove back into Deering, parked on the street and walked to the Deer Creek Lodge, a massive, three-story log structure with a restaurant. I went into the lobby. No one was at the desk, but I could hear talking from a back room. I picked up a stack of business cards from a holder, put them into my shirt pocket and left before anyone came out.

By then it was one o'clock and I was hungry. I walked around until I came to a small restaurant called the DeeLuxe. I went in. I'd have bet Paul Danner's ten grand that the owner was a woman named Dee.

Booths ran along one wall, tables along the other. At the far end was a sit-down counter. I didn't see any calendars, but

I suspected it would rate about a four on William Least Heat Moon's calendar-rating system for cafés. I was lunching late, and the place was nearly empty. I walked through to the counter and sat on a backless swivel stool with a vinyl seat on a wide chrome ring. A waitress came and stood across the counter from me.

She was blond, forty-something, and attractive in a seasoned kind of way; she looked like someone whose life had been about equal parts agreeable and disagreeable, but that the disagreeable parts had left her more wise than bitter. She didn't wear a name tag, maybe so male customers couldn't use her name to hit on her. She put a glass of ice water and a menu in front of me, photocopied sheets in a tri-panel plastic binder. She held a pad and pencil and waited while I studied the menu.

"What do you recommend?" I said.

"Nothing there I'm not proud to serve," she said. "The chicken-fried steak is popular. Any of the sandwiches'll fill you up. Potato chips and coleslaw go with. One substitution. We're out of the beef and noodles."

"I'll have a turkey melt and black coffee."

She went off. I swiveled on the stool and looked around. The artwork above the tables resembled the stuff on the walls of my cabin at the Whispering Pines—north country scenes with wildlife. A young couple, early season vacationers from the look of them, occupied a booth; a couple of guys in slacks and polo shirts at a table looked like they were either on their way to or from a round of golf.

The waitress brought my coffee and went back into the kitchen. She brought me an oval platter with a sandwich on rye bread and some potato chips and a small bowl of coleslaw. She went to check on the other customers then returned and topped off my coffee without my having to ask.

As I blackened the coleslaw with pepper, she leaned against the counter and took the order pad from a pocket of her apron and the pencil from behind her ear and did some addition.

"I'm looking for somebody," I said to her.

"Ain't we all," she said with a wry, tired smile.

I pulled the picture of Eric Danner out of my shirt pocket and showed it to her. I had cropped it with scissors, leaving only the head, so that I could carry it around more easily.

"Ever see him in here or around town? He might have some facial hair now."

She took the picture and looked at it then gave it back to me.

"Can't say I have."

"Would you tell me if you had?"

She gave me a look. "Depends on why you want to know."

"He's missing, and his dad would like to find him."

"Is this kid in trouble?" she said.

"I don't know. He may be headed for it. I have reason to believe he's fallen in with some neo-Nazi skinheads around here."

A wall went up.

"I'm afraid I don't know nothing about that," she said.

I took out a Deer Creek Lodge business card and pushed it across the counter to her.

"I'm staying here," I said. "I'd appreciate it if you'd give me a call if you see the guy whose picture I showed you."

She didn't pick up the card from the counter and didn't say anything. Instead, by way of an answer, she tore off my ticket and covered the card with it. She didn't refill my coffee.

I finished and paid, but before leaving I went to the restroom. After emptying my bladder, I peeked in the single empty stall. The walls held graffiti; some of it referred to white power and North Star, some, in so many words, to the superior sexual performance of Aryan women. I went back out.

While I was in the restroom a cop had come in. He was maybe in his mid-thirties, tall and husky with ruddy cheeks and a blond brush of a mustache. His uniform was gray with green trim, and he wore a black cap with no logo or wording on the front. He and the waitress conversed with the casual familiarity of long-time acquaintances. The Deer Creek Lodge business card I had left on the counter was gone.

He left with a coffee to go. I went out behind him. He set off down the sidewalk on foot, slowly enough to sip coffee through the small hole in the plastic lid as he walked. I caught up with him.

"Good afternoon," I said.

He slowed then stopped and faced me.

"Good afternoon," he said. He came off as friendly and accessible, but I couldn't help but wonder if he was that way under orders from the Chamber of Commerce. His skin stretched dry and taut across high cheekbones; it was red, but not so much from the sun as from what seemed an internal heat that also flashed out of his eyes.

"Rick St. Clair," he said, offering his hand.

"Barry Pool."

"Welcome to Deering, Mr. Pool."

"Thanks. Maybe you can help me." I pulled out Eric Danner's picture and showed it to him. "I'm looking for this guy. I have reason to believe he came up here within the last couple of weeks and that there's a possibility that he's being held against his will. His name is Eric Danner."

With his free hand, he took the picture, gave it a close look, then handed it back to me.

"Do you mean he's been kidnapped?"

"Not that exactly, but he may not be free to leave if he wants to. Does the name North Star mean anything to you?"

He drew his brows together and pursed his lips, as if to try to squeeze something out of his memory. "North Star. You mean Polaris?"

He had to know that I knew that he was being coy.

"Eric Danner is Paul Danner's kid," I said.

"The guy running for the Senate?"

"He's my client. I'm a private detective from Milwaukee. Paul Danner came to me after his son dropped out of sight near the end of the school year at Marquette. He was a student there."

"You're a long ways from home," he said.

I didn't respond.

He said, "And you're not sure if this Eric Danner is in the area, and if he is whether or not he's here of his own free will?"

"That's right. He's twenty-one, and if he's here voluntarily, then I'm off the case. But I need to know."

"Well it just now occurs to me that I haven't answered your question about whether or not I've seen him. The answer is no, I haven't. And I'll be honest, if I do see him, I'm not sure I'll sound the alarm."

I got out another Deer Creek Lodge business card and handed it to him.

"I'm staying here," I said. "No need to sound the alarm if you see him, but I'd appreciate it if you let me know. He's probably driving a red SUV, a Ford Explorer."

St. Clair reared his head back and laughed out loud.

"If I had a nickel for every red SUV I see up here I could buy breakfast for you and me both at the DeeLuxe."

I put on a sheepish look.

"I wish you well in your search, Mr. Pool, and I hope you

enjoy our little town. Good day to you, sir."

I wasn't surprised or discouraged at the reactions I had got so far in Deering. Before beginning to ask questions, I had calculated for the possibility that some of the people I encountered might have direct or indirect connections to North Star, or at least be in sympathy with it, and that even those who didn't would be skittish on the subject, thinking that acknowledgment of North Star's presence would be bad for business. Rick St. Clair's position might be even more delicate. If North Star was a blight on the community he served and made his job harder, then he might have no reason to cover for them. But he also might not appreciate a city guy like me coming up and turning over rocks looking for worms.

I walked around town a while, asking about Eric Danner and leaving Deer Creek Lodge business cards with the proprietor of a gas station, a woman at the service desk in a grocery store, a liquor store clerk, and a woman behind the desk in the library. No one said they'd seen him.

It was late afternoon by the time I pulled onto the parking pad next to my cabin at the Whispering Pines. Inside, I took the phone book from the lower shelf of the beside table and opened it.

The Yellow Pages had no listing under White Supremacy or Skinhead or Nazi, neo- or otherwise. There was, however, a listing in the white pages for a Max Schale. I checked my pocket notebook. The address given matched the one I had copied from the magazine in Eric Danner's apartment. The phone number matched the one I called after getting it from information when I was there.

A little after five o'clock I drove a quarter mile down the road to the Loon Lake Tap, a log cabin bar with a Pabst Beer sign in the window. My intention was not actively to snoop, but to keep my ears open for any conversation that might be of interest.

A lot of bars can be divided into one of two types, the cave or the terrace. This one was a cave. The interior was dim; the theme, if it had one, was polished knotty pine and neon beer signs. I had a Pabst and a cheeseburger and french fries. Some locals were there. I half expected to get suspicious looks, but I got no looks at all. Almost as if in keeping with the atmosphere, the talk among the customers was low and muted; nothing I managed to make out was of any consequence to my case.

Around six-fifteen I drove back into Deering. I parked in a far corner of the lot at the Deer Creek Lodge, from which position I had a good view of the rest of the lot and the front entrance. I turned off the Jeep and waited and watched. It was close to the summer solstice, and it stayed light later in the north than in Milwaukee, so it would be a long time before I had the cover of darkness. I hoped no one would notice me sitting there and become suspicious.

Not much happened. A few vehicles pulled up with couples or foursomes, middle-aged or older. From the length of their stay, I assumed they were diners. Two or three cars disgorged overnight guests with luggage. Around eight o'clock they came.

Two young guys pulled up in a red SUV, parked near the lodge and got out. One wore a camouflage cap; the other, hatless, had a skinhead buzz; both wore jeans and tee shirts from under which their muscles bulged. One might have been Brad Schale, based on the description of him that Nancy Kane had given me, but I was too far away to see them very clearly, and I didn't use my binoculars out of concern for being conspicuous. They went inside. After only a couple of minutes, they came back out and drove off.

I got out and went into the lobby of the lodge and approached the desk. A woman was on duty.

"A friend of mine named Barry Pool is staying here," I said. "Can you ring him for me?"

She gave me a puzzled look.

"That's funny," she said. "Two guys were just in here asking for the same guy. There's no Barry Pool here, mister. Your friend must have told you the wrong place."

"Thanks anyway," I said, and left.

My gambit had told me what I suspected it might: I couldn't go around town openly looking for Eric Danner and voicing my suspicions about North Star's role in his disappearance without word getting to North Star.

I drove back to the Whispering Pines.

CHAPTER 10

I needed to locate the North Star compound, and I was convinced by then that if I asked around town I'd get stonewalled or sent chasing after a wild goose, so the next morning I drove up to Hurley, the Iron County seat, to have a look at plat maps in the courthouse. It didn't take me long to find some acreage owned by Russell Ingram off of a county road south of Deering, bounded on three sides by straight survey lines and, on the north, by the meandering shore of Crystal Lake.

I was back in Deering by noon, but still without a plan. On my way to the DeeLuxe for lunch, a red Ford Explorer passed me going the other way. I used a hardware store parking lot to make a quick U-turn and followed it. It entered the lot of Swann's Family Market, a mom-and-pop grocery store, and parked near the entrance. I pulled in and parked behind it, close enough to see the license plate. The number matched the one Paul Danner had given me for Eric's vehicle.

The guy who got out wasn't Eric Danner, I was sure of that. He wore camouflage cargo shorts and a tight-fitting black t-shirt. On his way into the store he looked around and rolled his shoulders, as if to say to anyone who might be watching, "Here's trouble, come and get it." I had a much closer look than I had at the guys at the Deer Creek Lodge the night before. He had an angry scowl on his face and tattoos on his arms. If he wasn't Brad Schale, I wasn't Barry Pool.

After about ten minutes inside, he came out carrying a twelve-pack of beer in one hand and a couple of plastic grocery bags in the other. He put them in the back of the Explorer, got in, and drove off. I followed.

Within minutes we were out in the countryside headed south. I stayed as far back as I could without losing him, making mental notes of road signs and prominent markers along the way.

I was about two hundred yards behind him on a straight, flat stretch when he crossed a bridge that traversed the narrow neck of a lake that dead-ended on the left and gradually widened on the right. On the other side of the bridge, he turned right onto a secondary road. I pulled over onto the shoulder and stopped before reaching the bridge. According to the map in Hurley, the North Star compound was on the other side of that lake. I turned onto a gravel road that followed the shore at least until it curved out of sight.

The lake was on my left, dense woods on the right. After going less than half a mile I pulled off onto a wide spot next to the lake. I backed up and turned around so that I was pointed toward the road I had turned off of.

I grabbed my binoculars and my camera, hung them both around my neck, and got out. I leaned back against the Jeep to steady myself. I looked through the binoculars across the lake and scanned.

On the other side, no more than a hundred yards away, the trees came up to the shore. Through the trees, maybe twenty yards back, were the nearest of a cluster of buildings. The largest looked like a state park lodge; a fieldstone foundation supported a log structure with dormers built into a steep roof covered with shake shingles. A porch with some outdoor furniture ran the entire length of the front. It might have been a church camp were it not for the flag high up on a pole—a swastika in a white circle on a red field.

The Ford Explorer was parked in front of the lodge. After a few minutes the guy I figured for Schale and another guy came out of the lodge together. They got in a car parked next to the Explorer and drove off.

My camera had a 70-300 zoom lens on it. I lifted it to my eye and snapped several shots, zooming in and out and panning. I took out my notebook and made some entries about my location and the route I had taken to get there.

As I was writing, the car that had driven off from the lodge came down the road, Brad Schale at the wheel. He pulled over and parked. Schale and his passenger got out and came toward me. Before they were too close to do something about it, I brought my camera up and aimed it at them and snapped a picture. They stopped as if frozen in place.

Schale regarded me with a malevolent sneer. He was shorter than me, but thicker and more muscular. The tattoos on both arms looked like stills from a horror movie.

"What do you think you're doing?" Schale said.

As he spoke I got out my cell phone and discovered to my relief that, unlike at the Whispering Pines, I had a signal. I punched in the number of the North Star compound and raised my right forefinger, by way of saying, "Phone conversation in progress, please wait"—as if I expected my visitors to observe the rules of courtesy. To my mild surprise, they did.

Someone at North Star answered. I said, loud enough for Schale to hear, "Russell Ingram, please." When I was told he wasn't available I said, eyes on the two guys there with me, "Then give him this message: I'm across the lake from you, with Brad Schale and another guy from your operation who look intent on doing me harm and running me off. I'd hate for that to happen. I'd hate even more to have to call Morris Dees if it does. He's awfully busy, as I'm sure you know."

I was put on hold. I heard talking in the background.

I felt like a gambler running a bluff. A few years earlier, in Idaho, Morris Dees, of the Southern Poverty Law Center, had put a white supremacist bunch out of business after their security guys shot at some people of color passing by on a public road. The case ended up in court, with the victims winning the entire property in a settlement. The main building was set ablaze in a fire-training exercise, after which some local Native Americans consecrated the grounds back to nature in a ritual ceremony. I had never met Morris Dees, but I was betting that the incident and his role in it were well known in the white supremacist community and had had a chilling effect. With my guns in the Jeep, I could only hope my gamble would pay off, and fast. What I saw across the lake suggested that it might: Someone came charging out the front door of the lodge and down the porch, got into a pickup and took off. I could see that Schale noticed, too. The phone line went dead.

"How do you know my name?" Schale said. "And why did you follow me?"

I said, "I'm bird watching. I came here hoping to add the Great Northern Redneck to my life list. It looks like my lucky day."

He came a step closer, but the anger on his face was diluted by confusion. The most he could come up with was, "Oh, yeah?"

I said, "Actually, I want to know if Eric Danner is free to come and go as he pleases or is being held against his will. If you tell me he's not over there"—I pointed across the lake—"I'll call you a liar, and you'll have to deal with that. If you admit he is but insist on not letting me see him, then *I'll* have to deal with *that*. And I will."

The pickup came down the road and stopped alongside us. The driver said to Schale through the open window, "The old man says to call it off and come back."

Schale spat in the dirt. "*The old man!*"

He looked at me and jabbed the air with a finger.

"You and me ain't done."

He and the other guy got back in their car and drove off. The pickup followed.

As they were leaving, I took pictures of their license plates and made sure they saw me doing so. I couldn't imagine any value in having that information, but felt an impish desire to ruffle the feathers of the Great Northern Redneck.

CHAPTER 11

Near the end of my encounter with Brad Schale, I had made brave albeit vague talk about what I would do if he denied me access to Eric Danner. If he had replied, as my gang of friends used to say when I was a kid, "You and what army?" I wouldn't have had a good answer. I was an army of one, which is to say no army at all, and no match for an unknown number of fanatics on their turf.

Had I been going up against only Brad Schale, I'd have found the task less daunting but no less distasteful. He was a villainous-looking fellow, with vicious eyes and facial hair that suggested a werewolf in the early stages of transformation.

I spent the next few days going over the same ground, returning at different times to that spot across the lake from North Star's compound, watching through my binoculars and taking more pictures. I sometimes heard gunfire, some of it coming from automatic weapons, none of it aimed in my direction. The only difference from that first day was that nobody came over to hassle me. My Morris Dees gambit might have afforded me some protection, but I wasn't convinced it would do so if I escalated my level of risk. And without a break of some kind, it looked like that's what I'd have to do if I wanted to make progress on the case. On trips into Deering for groceries or a meal I kept an eye out for Eric Danner, hoping I might get lucky and catch him alone and come away satisfied that he was thinking and acting for himself.

My route from the spot across the lake from the North Star compound to the Whispering Pines took me through town. After my fourth straight day next to the lake, as I rounded a long curve on my way back into Deering, I spotted someone on foot on my side of the road, going in my direction. It was a female. She shot a wary look over her shoulder as I got closer and seemed to position herself to run for it if need be. After giving me another look, she turned to face me and, still on the move only now backpedaling, she extended her right arm and held out her thumb. A few feet past her I pulled over and stopped. In the passenger side mirror I could see her approach. When she got up to the door I powered the window down.

"Want a lift?"

She looked at me, weighing the risk. I remembered what Nancy Kane had said about me.

"I promise I'm safe," I said.

"That's what you'd say if you weren't, just to get me in."

"Probably," I said. "But in this case it's true, which is also what I'd say if it wasn't. Suit yourself." I shifted into drive.

A pickup approached from behind us. She spotted it.

"Wait."

She climbed in and closed the door and looked at me with resentment, blaming me for her lack of options.

She wore tight, faded jeans, running shoes, a yellow t-shirt, and a Brewers cap. She was young and pretty in an uncomplicated kind of way, with straight brown hair to the shoulder, sparkling brown eyes and pouty lips. She had a bruise on her left cheek and more on her forearms.

"I'm Barry," I said.

"That's nice."

I drove off. After a while I said, "How do I know *you're* safe."

"You don't." Her eyes flashed mischievous pleasure in the role reversal.

I said, "Where are you headed?"

The question seemed to catch her off guard.

"Um, town." She was trying to sound decisive and not pulling it off.

"Me, too. You're in luck."

"Are you from around here?" she said.

"I'm from Milwaukee."

"What brings you north?"

"Trouble."

"I've seen some of that."

"Most people have," I said.

"What kind of trouble?"

"I'm still trying to find out," I said, "along with how much. It involves a young guy named Eric Danner." I pulled the photo from my shirt pocket and held it out for her to see. "He'd be a little older than you. His father would like to know where he is and if he's okay. He may have some facial hair now. Have you seen him?"

She looked at the picture then looked straight ahead.

"I reckon you found it," she said.

"Found what?"

"Trouble."

CHAPTER 12

I finally got her to tell me that her name was Lisa. On the way to Deering, whenever a vehicle approached from the opposite direction she scrunched down in the seat and lowered her head so the bill of her cap hid her face.

"Are you hungry?" I said as we came to the edge of town.

She gave a quick, desperate nod. I drove to the DeeLuxe and parked in front. I started to get out.

"I don't want to go in there," she said. "I'm from around here. People know me, and they're not all friends. And Brad and his buddies might come to town looking for me."

"Brad Schale?"

"How do you know?"

"We've met. He's connected to the guy I'm looking for. Did he give you those bruises?"

She didn't answer.

"I'll be honest," she said. "When you picked me up I wasn't necessarily heading for town. I don't know where I want to go. I don't *have* anywhere to go. I just had to get away from Brad and that place. If you don't want me around, I guess there's not much I can do about it. But could you at least stake me to something to eat? Not here, though. There's a grocery store pretty close."

"Swann's?"

She nodded, then cringed. "I can't pay or anything."

We went to Swann's and parked.

I said, "I'll go in. You can stay here and try to stay out of sight. Anything in particular you want to eat?"

"Yeah, food."

I took the keys to the Jeep with me.

At the deli section in Swann's I picked up four sandwiches wrapped in cellophane and two paper cups of coffee from an urn. I made my way around and grabbed potato chips, a box of snack crackers, a bag of apples, a bunch of bananas, a six-pack of Cokes in cans. I took it all out in plastic bags, except for the coffees, which were in a molded tray. I'm not sure why, but I was surprised to find Lisa still waiting there in the Jeep. I opened the door, handed the stuff into the space between the front seats and got in.

"Help yourself to coffee or a Coke," I said.

She took a coffee.

I said, "Do you want to eat something right here right now, eat as we drive, or go somewhere else?"

"Where would we go?"

"You tell me. You know this area better than I do."

"I wouldn't feel safe anywhere we can be seen," she said.

"I'm staying in a cabin at the Whispering Pines outside of town. It's ten minutes away."

"I know the place."

I said, "We may be able to help each other. You need to lie low until you figure some things out, and I need information about Eric Danner. The cabin I'm in is behind the main building, out of sight of the road. We can go there and eat and then decide what to do."

She squinted at me sideways.

"How do I know you're not some kind of rapist ax-murderer?"

"You don't."

She thought about that for a moment then said, "I guess I don't have much choice but to trust you."

"We're trusting each other," I said. "And as long as you're with me I'm making myself a target of Brad Schale and whoever else might be looking for you. You don't have to say thanks, but in return I want information. And that's all I want. Which is probably what I'd say if I wanted something else. I hope you're at least eighteen."

She gave me an impish, enigmatic smile.

"I can wait to eat till we get to the Whispering Pines," she said. She scrunched down in the seat again and sipped coffee under the bill of her cap.

"Do you have a last name?" I said as we drove away.

"It's Moody." She wrinkled her nose and gave me a mischievous look. "Rhymes with cutie. I didn't catch yours."

"It's Pool," I said. "Barry Pool." I looked over at her. She was a cutie all right, and possibly jail bait, and more trouble than I needed. But she seemed desperate, and I would have felt like a heel ditching her. "Rhymes with fool."

CHAPTER 13

At the cabin we dug into the food.

"You must have left in a hurry," I said. "You don't even have a change of clothes."

"I was tired of being hit."

She pulled back her hair on the left side to reveal purplish skin along her jaw.

"By Brad Schale?"

"Yeah."

"Is he your boyfriend?"

She made a face. "In his dreams and my nightmares."

"Why did he hit you?"

"Because I can't stand cruelty and I told him in front of the others that I thought he was sick for what he was doing to Eric Danner. That was one reason. He also smacked me once for saying Hitler was stupid for invading Russia."

"What did he do to Eric Danner?"

"They have this good-cop, bad-cop routine when they want to break a guy. They mock him, beat him, keep him awake. Then somebody steps in and stops it, and they gradually build him up again. They tell him how valuable he can be to the movement and try to give him a sense of belonging. If it works he's theirs to use any way they want. In Eric's case, though, they went even farther."

She cringed at the memory.

"They had this mock trial and sentenced him to hang."

"What was his crime?"

"Doubt. Lack of commitment. They tied his hands behind him and led him out into the woods. Brad made me go out with them and watch. He said it was for being so mouthy. They showed him the tree limb they were going to hang him from and told him he'd hang there for everybody to see until the crows picked the flesh off his bones. They threw a rope over the limb with a noose at one end, put a black hood over his head and the noose around his neck then started pulling on the other end until the slack was gone and he was up on his toes. He was shaking and crying hysterically. I almost puked. I'm sure the whole thing was a setup, but for a while they had me wondering. Then another guy stepped in and told Eric he didn't have to die like that if he'd be a soldier for the cause. Eric was blubbering and couldn't talk, but he nodded. They lowered him down and took off the noose and the hood. They had to hold him up on both sides when they walked him back to the church."

"Church?"

"The main hall doubles as a church. There's all these Nazi and white power symbols and stuff in there, plus a cross. Brad and his faction could care less about the religion part, though."

The word *faction* piqued my interest. I remembered Schale's anger by the lake at being reined in by "the old man."

"There's division on the compound?"

"Big time," she said. "Brad and some others, all young guys, have pretty much taken over. They've been using the Internet to organize with a bunch of other groups. People are coming and going all the time. Ex-Marines. Guys from Canada. They even brought in a guy from Germany, Dieter Strassman, to do training in weapons and tactics."

That explained the gunfire I heard from across the lake.

"Talk about getting the hen house in an uproar. That was another reason I got hit. Brad could tell I was checking Dieter out and he got jealous, even though he had no claim on me.

"Women aren't allowed into the inner circle, so I'm not sure what they're up to, but something big is in the works. Big in their eyes, anyway. It's pathetic to hear them at times. They talk like they're going to overthrow the U.S. government any day now and march out to conquer the world for the white race by next Christmas. They have no patience for the older generation. A while back they ran up a Nazi flag and took down the one that Mr. Ingram designed, and nobody challenged them.

"Anyway, when I told Brad that I thought what he did to Eric was sick, he hit me. That was yesterday. I decided not to take it anymore. I stayed overnight in the dorm building I shared with some of the other women, then took off on foot when everybody was in the main hall for lunch."

"Did anyone try to stop you?"

"Nobody knew. I slipped out the back and followed a path through the woods to the road and walked until you came by. You said you wanted information. There it is. But I'm not just repaying you for picking me up. I'd love to get back at Brad. If you want the truth, I'm not into the whole Aryan Woman thing. I ended up there because my dad kicked me out of the house and I had nowhere else to go and I knew some girls that were there. I played along and blended in, but I don't like what they're up to, the young guys anyway. They're getting jacked on meth—Brad and some of the others bring it in from somewhere—and they're itching for a fight. They'll self-destruct, but not before taking some innocent people down first."

I thought for a moment then said, "What are your plans?"

She looked desperate and forlorn.

"I don't *have* any plans. I have no place to go. I was hoping you'd let me stay here."

"If Brad Schale and his boys come looking for you and find you with me, that could interfere with my work. It could even interfere with my plans to live longer."

"You said this place ought to be safe. Besides, we could have a good time." She reached across the small table and touched my hand. "And not just because I'm grateful. You're not bad looking, and you're put together nice."

"I'm flattered, but no thanks."

"I don't get it. Guys want me. I don't have a disease or anything. Are you gay?"

"At the National Bureau of Standards there's a picture of me that's used to illustrate the concept of straightness."

"That's pretty lame."

"Okay. Let's just say I have old-fashioned ideas about love and sex and marriage. I also have a part-time girlfriend."

She pouted.

"You can stay for now," I said. "We'll take it a day at a time. No guarantees, though, except I promise not to send you out alone to face harm. Deal?"

"Deal, but you're a strange one. If you change your mind about the other stuff, let me know."

"I'll do that."

That night I took the bed nearest the door. The cabin didn't have air conditioning, so I opened windows. A breeze came through, and I learned why the place was called the Whispering Pines. As I lay there awake, Lisa softly snoring in the other bed, I imagined hearing the whisperings of a murderous band of skinhead thugs, Brad Schale among them, as they crept up to the cabin to dispatch me in my sleep.

CHAPTER 14

Lisa had nothing with her in the way of toiletries or a change of clothes when I picked her up. I got her through a couple of days with some things of mine—t-shirts and a pair of sport shorts that she cinched tight—and an extra toothbrush from Vern's office. Figuring it would be futile to try to hide her presence from Vern and his housekeeping staff, I told him I had a female guest and offered to pay more. Vern, whose days of sexual pleasure were probably long past, leered and gave me a knowing wink and said it would be okay.

Later she got some of her clothes and other personal things by calling a female friend on the compound, who delivered them to the cabin while I was away. When I scolded her for committing a potentially serious breach of security, she swore that her friend could be trusted. Nevertheless, I gave her strict instructions against answering or using the phone, lest she reveal her whereabouts and word get to the wrong people. I might as well have given the sun strict instructions not to rise in the morning and set in the evening. At least she seemed content to stay in the cabin while I was out snooping or in town. From her talk, which was more or less incessant, I gathered that she spent her time watching television, especially old movies, painting and repainting her finger- and toenails, and working crossword puzzles in the newspapers I picked up.

Intermittently, I had been making calls to Paul Danner using the cell phone number he gave me, to apprise him of my progress, which wasn't much. He had said it would be a direct line to him, but that turned out not to be exactly the case. As often as not, my calls were intercepted and handled by Tim Reed, his staff chief, who said Danner had briefed him on the case and authorized him to relay messages from me. After learning what I did from Lisa, I told Reed that Eric might be undergoing a kind of brainwashing—I left out the story of the mock hanging—but frankly admitted that I was at a loss for how to get to him. I later regretted sharing that information, since it might serve to ratchet up the pressure on me to get to Eric and get him out of there.

Sure enough, when I returned to the Whispering Pines one afternoon Lisa said someone representing Paul Danner had called and that Danner needed to talk to me. I returned the call and as usual got Tim Reed. I expected him to ask about who answered the phone in the cabin, but he didn't. He said Danner was planning a swing through the north, from Green Bay to Superior with stops in between, and wanted me to come down to Rhinelander for a meeting around lunch time the next day. We set it up for twelve thirty.

Rhinelander was two hours away. It felt good to get clear of

Deering and the Whispering Pines and be about other business than that of spying on Skinhead Nation. I got into town early and bought a copy of Rhinelander's *Daily News* from a street box and took it to a coffee shop.

The coverage in the paper was mostly local and of little interest to me, except for a front-page piece on a shooting in the parking lot of an Indian casino on the Lac du Flambeau Reservation. According to witnesses, around seven-thirty the previous night a guy had pulled up in the lot in a pickup and fired at random with a handgun at patrons on their way in and out of the casino. An elderly man was killed and three other people wounded. The perpetrator got away and a search was on. What witnesses there were had been too busy scrambling for cover to come up with a good description of the shooter—only that he was white and the truck was green.

An inside page devoted to state and national news ran a few column inches on the Travis Isely case in Milwaukee. The police involved in the shooting had been cleared of wrongdoing, and Milwaukee's black community was in an uproar.

I drove around and found Holland's, the restaurant where I was to meet Paul Danner. The place was about two-thirds full of what looked like downtown workers—clerks and secretaries and lawyers and shopkeepers. Before the hostess got to me I spotted Paul Danner in a booth off to the right, like any other citizen. He waved me over.

Two others were with him, a young female on the inside of the bench seat next to Danner and a guy by himself opposite. He and Danner were in shirtsleeves and tie. I sat in the empty space. Danner did introductions. The guy next to me was Tim Reed.

"I feel like we've met," he said as we shook hands.

He was younger than Danner and shared his fraternity-guy

good looks, but had a keener eye. The female was introduced only as Joy. She had a stenographer's pad open in front of her on the table and a pencil in one hand. A waitress came over and took our orders—sandwich platters for all except Joy, who had only a diet cola.

Danner said, "I believe Tim told you that this was to be a briefing session, an update if you will."

As he spoke he did a quick visual check with Reed. In my peripheral vision, I detected an affirmative nod.

"That's my understanding," I said.

Danner said, "Tim's report of your last phone conversation was a little alarming. I'm curious to know about the methods these people might be using to . . ." He stopped and looked across at Reed.

Reed said, "You used the word *brainwashing*."

I gave it to them straight, as much as I knew from Lisa, including her account of the aborted hanging. I attributed much of what I told them to what I described as an "inside source" that I had found by sheer chance.

"It's not likely that they intended to hang him," I said. "The whole exercise seems to have been designed to break him down. It's safe to guess that they at least want him to believe as they believe; quite possibly they have a mission for him. But what kind, I can't say. My source thinks they're planning something. She says there's lots of coming and going on the compound of people from like-minded groups, including a guy from Germany who's conducting weapons training."

As I spoke it occurred to me for the first time that Eric might be the guy in the green pickup who had made the hit on the Indian Casino that was in the morning news, but I didn't bring it up. If it was him, the matter was out of any of our hands; if it wasn't him, I saw no need to cause undue alarm.

I said, "The question uppermost in my mind is the one I made a point of when you hired me: Is Eric there against his will? My best guess is that the terms of that question no longer apply. I think he probably came up voluntarily, at least more or less, but that he may no longer have a will to call upon."

Reed said, "If that's the case, then, technically speaking, he's not there *against* his will."

It struck me as an odd observation, one that didn't acknowledge Eric's welfare as the highest priority. I sensed that Reed was trying to steer the conversation in a direction that he had wanted it to go in all along.

I said, "*Technically speaking*, that's true, but I'm afraid it ignores some ugly facts."

Paul Danner looked from Reed to me then back to Reed. A moment of silence ensued. Joy sipped cola through a straw, pencil poised.

Reed said, "You referred to your source as *she*."

He waited for me to explain. My mind ran ahead to their reaction to my telling them that my source was a young female, possibly underage, whom I had picked up alongside the road and who had been kicked out of her house by her father for who knew what—pregnancy or substance abuse or both, they might well speculate, as I had—and with whom, from their point of view, I appeared to be shacking up, all expenses paid. I gave it to them, slanting the facts in my favor by emphasizing her value as a source.

Reed said, "Has it occurred to you to wonder about her credibility?"

"Yes it has."

Reed started to speak, but I cut him off and addressed Paul

Danner.

"I'm convinced she has no reason to lie to me or to make the story up. I have no illusions about how she's lived her life and what that says about her judgment, but I think she's more mixed up than bad and don't suspect her of having a hidden agenda. I believe what she's told me is accurate and potentially useful, if I can find a way to use it. Either way, it's the best I've been able to come up with. What I don't know is what my next move is."

I looked at Danner. Danner looked at Reed.

Using a concessionary tone that struck me as a transparent attempt at taking me into his confidence and making me feel privileged for doing so, Reed said, "Our problem, Mr. Pool, is not that we don't believe you but that we do. We seriously doubt that Eric's mother has his welfare at heart and may even be behind the events you've described. All of which means that Eric may be damaged and dangerous and less of a threat if he's confined to that compound than off of it."

I said, "It sounds like my orders have been changed from rescue to containment."

Perhaps not ready to forfeit all decision-making to his staff chief, Paul Danner looked at me and said, "What do you think is best?"

The question was so vague and inapt as to be meaningless, and I was almost lost for words.

"Best for whom? Best in terms of what outcome?"

Danner blinked and bit his lower lip and looked at Reed.

Reed said, "We have to think of the greater good. Mr. Danner's election to the Senate could tip the balance for a Republican majority." Danner nodded. "Which in turn could lead to policies and laws that in our estimation will make this a better and safer country, the world a better and safer place."

There it was: Civilization as we knew it might rise or fall depending on what I did in the next few days.

Reed said, "If Eric gets off that compound and does something awful . . . Surely you can imagine the negative publicity and what our opponents will try to make of it."

The waitress came and asked if we wanted dessert. By then I wouldn't have been surprised to see Danner look to Reed for an answer. But he didn't have to. Reed declined for all of us.

When she left, Reed said, "We'd like you to be our eyes and ears up here while we get on with the campaign. Go back and watch the situation. If at all possible, try to get to Eric and discern his state of mind, but not at the risk of tipping the balance and sending him over the edge, wherever that might be. We realize that containment, as you put it, may be too much to ask. If Eric leaves the compound, alone or with company, let us know. Follow him if you can and keep us apprised of his movements."

I sat and thought. Joy waited for my answer.

"I'll do my best," I said.

"That's all we can ask," Danner said. He looked to Reed for affirmation.

As we rose to part company, Danner looked at me with a kind of pleading uncertainty. I had the feeling that he wanted me to take it from him and turn it into decisiveness. Reed nodded at me with complete certainty as we shook hands, as if he had full faith that I knew exactly what to do and would do it.

CHAPTER 15

I knew I had been up north too long when I caught myself thinking that in returning to the cabin at the Whispering Pines I was returning home. On the way, I listened to local news on a radio station out of Minocqua. It included a late-breaking story of a shooting, that morning, of some Hmong immigrants at an Asian grocery store in Wausau. None had died, but two were in critical condition. Witnesses, the victims among them, described the shooter as a young white male driving a green truck. The state police and local agencies were conducting a manhunt.

When I went into the cabin, Lisa was there, sitting cross-legged on a bed in panties and t-shirt, painting her toenails and watching local television news coverage of the shootings at the Indian casino and in Wausau. Unabashed at my seeing her so scantily attired, she looked at me and said, "It's starting."

We compared stories—what I had read in Rhinelander

about the casino attack, the news I'd heard on the radio from Wausau, and what she had picked up from television.

I said, "Could it be Eric?"

"I doubt it. There was this guy who came a few weeks earlier than Eric that drove a green pickup. They gave him the treatment, not the same as Eric's, but bad enough. I'm guessing it's him."

"Is this the kind of thing they're preparing Eric for?"

Lisa shrugged. "What else?"

At some point I couldn't put my finger on, I had come to think of Eric Danner as a victim—of our culture of divorce, Paul Danner's political ambitions, his mother's fanaticism. My trip to Rhinelander had reinforced that thinking. My conversation there earlier that day with Paul Danner and Tim Reed, and their latest instructions, now seemed irrelevant.

I said, "How do people get onto the compound in vehicles? Can I simply drive up to the lodge?"

"The only way in or out by car is through the main gate. It's usually open during the day."

"On one of my stakeouts across the lake, around five o'clock, about a dozen vehicles came by from down the road. A few minutes later most of them appeared on the compound."

"They were getting off their shift at the timber company. A bunch of them work there. What are you planning?"

"Foolishness."

That night I was too keyed up to sleep well. The next morning I went into town for breakfast around nine o'clock, before Lisa woke up. I hung around town for a while, mostly at the library, trying to occupy my mind with anything but the task ahead.

I returned to the cabin around mid-afternoon. Lisa was bored and pouty and grew testy when I insisted on changing TV channels from the soap opera she was watching to CNN. I wanted to see if the guy in the green pickup was national news, and if so, what he was up to lately. After a full news cycle, I could see that he wasn't.

Milwaukee was, though. Civil rights leaders from around the country—the ones Jill had mentioned that night at Delaney's, along with a few others—had announced their intention to converge on the city in about a week for a rally and march to protest what they called the injustice done in the Travis Isely case and the MPD's all but official policy of police brutality.

Under other circumstances that news would have grabbed my attention and held it, but I was too strung out from a bad night's sleep and fretting too much over what I faced later that day to give it much thought.

I gave the remote back to Lisa and asked her to keep the volume down. She turned the TV off instead and huffed into the bathroom. I stretched out but couldn't sleep.

When the time came for me to make my move I realized that I had to decide what to do with my guns. I didn't want them on my person on the compound because I didn't want to give the skinheads a pretext to kill me and claim self-defense. But neither did I want to leave them in the cabin with Lisa there. I stowed them out of reach and out of sight in the rear of the Jeep.

I was back at my stakeout spot at four thirty, watching through binoculars. Around five I heard the first of the vehicles approach from down the road. I got in the Jeep and started it and put it in gear. Two or three cars came by. Then a pickup passed that I had seen drive onto the compound on an earlier stakeout. Before the next vehicle came into view from around the curve, I pulled out and got in behind the pickup.

We turned right at the county road, drove across the bridge and turned right again onto the narrow asphalt lane that led to the compound. The gate came into view, open and unattended. The guy ahead of me went through. I followed.

I was in.

CHAPTER 16

I parked in front of the lodge and got out. More vehicles came in behind me and drove to other buildings. A few people were about on foot, but none close by, and they paid me no mind. Given what Lisa had said about outsiders coming and going, they might have thought I was just another friendly Nazi visiting from out of town. I went up onto the porch and through the front door without knocking.

I was in a large gathering room. Exposed timbers supported a high ceiling from the center of which hung a black, wrought-iron candle chandelier. Couches and padded chairs and low tables were clustered to form conversation areas. A stone fireplace was on my right. Mounted on the chimney above the mantle was a photo of Adolf Hitler in profile, looking off into the twilight of his thousand-year Reich.

The smell of food cooking came through a door that led

to what looked like a dining hall. Two long corridors went off in the same direction from opposite corners of the wall across from the fireplace. An old man came into the room from one of them. He was tall but stooped, with a heavy, ponderous air about him. He looked like a bloodhound, with big ears and a long face that sagged under the eyes and at the jowls. I recognized him as Russell Ingram from his picture on North Star's website that I had seen in Eric's apartment. He gave me a cheerless smile that exuded condescension and paternalism, and said in a sonorous baritone,

"Who might you be, and what's your business here?"

I was off balance. All my training told me that as a guest and in the presence of an elderly gentleman I was obliged to be polite and deferential, but I couldn't quite accept that the rules of courtesy applied to Nazis.

I said, "My name's Barry Pool and I'm looking for Eric Danner."

He didn't answer. A woman came into the room and stood next to him, her eyes on me.

"Frieda, this gentleman is asking after Eric."

Her presence unsettled me even more than I already was. She had unruly hair and squinting eyes that suggested obsession and paranoia. I found it hard to imagine that she and Paul Danner had once been husband and wife.

She looked straight at me but spoke to her father in a wheezy croak:

"Has he said why?"

Ingram raised his eyebrows at me.

I said, "I want to know if he's free to come and go as he pleases. I'd like to hear what he'd say about where he wants to be and what he wants to do when there's nobody else around to listen."

Russell Ingram said, "Why?"

"Because his father wants to know. I'm working for him."

Frieda Schale's eyes squirmed. She said, "You're too late. Eric's gone."

It sounded like a lie, made up on the spot to get rid of me.

I said, "Gone for the day or for good?"

"For good."

"How do I know that's true?"

She bristled. "I resent you coming here and calling me a liar."

"Strictly speaking, I didn't."

Two men came into the room together. One was middle-aged. The other was Brad Schale. Seeing me, he stopped and sneered, exuding aggression and violence. The older guy hung back. I saw enough of Brad Schale in his face to infer that he was his father, Max Schale, Frieda's current husband.

"Is there a problem?" Brad Schale said.

He squared off on me, wanting the answer to be yes. Ingram made a slight gesture with one hand that held him in place. Max Schale wanted to be somewhere else. Frieda Schale blinked and squinted. I had a feeling the scene was a window on the dynamic at North Star.

"No there isn't," Ingram said. "Mr. Pool was just leaving."

I wasn't ready to leave. I wasn't satisfied that I had been told the truth. By way of stirring the waters to see what rose to the surface, I thought of goading Brad Schale by telling him that Lisa and I had been sharing a cabin, but I didn't want to set Lisa up for a rough time later. Instead, in the same goading spirit, I said to Frieda Schale,

"At least satisfy my curiosity: Does Eric's being raised in

part by a Jewish stepmother make him damaged goods, and thus expendable, like the guy in the green pickup?"

A young man in shirt and tie and a swastika armband leaned into the room from the dining hall and said, "Mr. Ingram, dinner is ready."

Ingram turned his head toward him and said, "We'll be right there." To me he said, "It's time for you to leave. I suggest you do so while you still can."

I said, "I'll have a look around first."

I went through the front door and onto the porch. Someone came out behind me. I turned in time to see that it was Brad Schale, but not in time to stop him from kicking me down the steps.

I got up to my hands and knees, but before I could get to my feet Schale was in front of me. He had a gun in his hand; he used it to deliver a blow to the top of my head. I grabbed for his legs, but he jumped out of reach and I ended up sprawled. I tried getting up, but he got around behind me and straddled my back and rode me down. My face was in the grass. He put the muzzle of his gun to the back of my head. I heard the hammer cock.

"Say your prayers," Schale said.

I had already started—*Hail Mary, full of grace* . . .

"That's enough, Brad," Russell Ingram said from the porch. "Let him go."

Schale got up. I tried to, but he kicked me back down.

"I'm not through with you," he said, and went up the steps and inside.

Ingram said, "You'd do well to leave this area, Mr. Pool, and soon. I'm unable to guarantee that I can rein in all the forces at work here."

He went in to dinner.

I struggled to my feet and into the driver's seat of the Jeep. I sat and let my head clear a moment and examined myself in the mirror. Schale's grip on the gun seemed to have blunted the blow, and I didn't appear to be bleeding or lacerated under my hair. I wasn't convinced that Eric had left the compound, but I was in no position to press the issue. I'd at least have to wait until my head cleared before trying another approach, maybe bringing local law enforcement down on the place over my having been assaulted, if I could convince myself that local law enforcement would back me. Maybe I'd call Morris Dees after all. I wasn't up to driving, but I drove off anyway. The gate was still open. I decided to return to the cabin, but made sure first that no one was following me.

Back at the cabin, Lisa was gone, but her things were still there. That worried me. I trusted her intentions but not her judgment, and my mind ran to the possibility of coming under siege if she inadvertently divulged my whereabouts to the wrong people.

I went into the bathroom and dampened a washcloth. I lay on the bed and applied it to my scalp and turned on the television. I was exhausted enough that I drifted in and out of sleep despite the pain I was in.

At ten o'clock, I watched local news on a station from Minocqua. The lead story was the guy in the green pickup. He had made his way down to the University of Wisconsin campus in Stevens Point and executed drive-by shootings on a couple of minorities he happened upon, one a student, the other a faculty member out for a walk with his family. The student was in serious condition in the hospital with a wound to the shoulder. The faculty member was dead, killed in front of his wife and little girl. This time, though, the cops managed to corner the perpetrator at a roadblock outside of town and killed him in a shootout when he made a stand that the TV reporter on the scene called "suicidal." He was ID'd as Adam Widger, twenty-five, originally from Ashland but with no known current address. He had methamphetamine on him, and, according to police speculation pending autopsy results, probably in him.

The next thing I knew I was waking up to the sound of Lisa coming in. The clock on the table between the beds read 11:37. She was drunk. When I asked where she had been she said she had got bored and walked down to the Loon Lake Tavern, where, presumably, they hadn't quibbled about her age.

"You put us both at risk by doing that," I said.

She waved it off. "Nobody was there that knows me. Except the bartender, my uncle."

"Did you tell him where you were staying?"

She grinned drunkenly and put a hand over her mouth, as if to hold in what had already escaped.

"I guess I might've. He's cool, though. What happened to you?"

I told her about my encounter with Brad Schale.

"Now you know what I mean about that guy. And you didn't even get to see Eric."

"How do you know that?"

"Right after you left you got a phone call from Nancy somebody in Milwaukee. I forget her last name. She said she tried your cell but couldn't get through, so she called here. It sounded kind of urgent. She said to tell you Eric's back in his apartment."

CHAPTER 17

I was in no shape to spring into action, much less drive long distance, but I immediately began gathering up my things and loading them into the Jeep. I told Lisa on the run that I was done there and heading back to Milwaukee.

"What about me?" she said with a pout, sitting on the side of a bed.

"This morning I paid in advance for a few more days. As far as I'm concerned you can stay here through then if it's okay with Vern. After that, you're on your own."

The pout was still in place. I sat on the bed next to her and gave her a hug with one arm.

"We'll always have the Whispering Pines," I said.

She rolled her eyes.

I stopped by the office on my way out. It was dark and the door was locked, but I could see the shifting blue light of a television from a back room. I pounded on the door. In slippers and sleepwear, Vern came and opened, smelling of beer. I told him I was leaving and asked his indulgence on the arrangement with Lisa. He gave me another wink that I took for both consent to that arrangement and appreciation for the great time I must have had with her.

At the first convenience store I came to I stopped for gas, coffee, and snacks. Except for stops for more coffee and to go to the bathroom, I made the trip straight through, without getting stopped for speeding, and unlocked the front door of my house on the East Side around six in the morning.

The post office had been holding my mail, so I had none to sort. My answering machine had some messages, but I didn't play them. I found it hard to resist calling Nancy Kane for a report on Eric Danner, even harder to resist driving right over there and knocking on her door. But I needed sleep and didn't want to disturb her at that hour, so I went to bed without setting an alarm.

I awoke around eight-thirty, confused and disoriented and wondering why the cabin at the Whispering Pines looked so different. When I figured out where I was and remembered how I got there, an unfocused sense of urgency flooded into me. My head hurt where Brad Schale had clobbered me, but only superficially, without throbbing. I showered and dressed, made toast and coffee, then called Nancy Kane. She answered on the second ring.

"It's Barry Pool. I'm back in town. Is Eric still there?"

"As far as I know, he is. I haven't talked to him, though. You can come over if you want. I'm free till noon."

"Maybe later. I need to work another angle first. I'll check back with you."

I needed to know if Paul Danner knew of Eric's return to Milwaukee. In Rhinelander he had indicated that after his stop in Superior he'd come down the western side of the state then spend a couple of days in Madison. I tried his cell phone. Tim Reed answered.

"What's up, Pool?"

"Eric's back in Milwaukee."

"We know. He called. I probably don't need to tell you how relieved his father is."

"I need to see him."

"Eric?"

"No, his dad. Is he within reach of you right now? Can I talk to him?"

"What about?"

"It's about Eric. Where are you?"

"We're in La Crosse. Eric's back and is fine. And you've been paid. What's left to talk about?"

I didn't think I could reveal more without the sense that I was revealing it to the wrong person under the wrong circumstances.

"No offense, but this is for Paul Danner's ears only. And it's urgent. If you play gatekeeper and don't convey this to your boss you won't be serving his interests. What happened to your concern about what Eric might do if he got off the compound?"

"That was before Eric returned and talked to his dad. Paul is convinced he's fine and that there's nothing to worry about. He's his father, he ought to know."

"What's your next move?" I said.

"We'll be in Madison this afternoon."

"Exactly where and when?"

"If it's absolutely necessary, you can catch us on the Capitol grounds around three o'clock, assuming we're on schedule. We should be able to fit you in after Paul makes an appearance there, but only briefly. But if this is more stuff from that source of yours, you'll be wasting your time and ours. You might want to think about the impression you're going to leave on an important client and what kind of reference he'd give to anyone that asked about you."

"I'll see you in Madison."

CHAPTER 18

A three o'clock appointment in Madison left me time to rest a little and do some things that might make me feel normal again. I went to pick up my mail at the post office, where I did a quick sort-and-pitch, then returned home with what remained and went through it, reading some and separating the rest into piles. I played the messages on my answering machine, none of which needed immediate responses. I partially caught up on the accumulated newspapers then tried taking a nap, but was too wired to sleep. I lay there anyway, trying to force my mind and body to rest. Before leaving, I brewed a pot of brutally strong coffee and poured it into my Aladdin, then took off for Madison, making it in about an hour and a half.

I parked on a side street near the Capitol and walked over and joined a moderate-sized crowd on the east side of the building where Paul Danner was speaking. When he finished he came down to work the crowd. I made my way up to the sawhorse barrier. He was shaking my hand before he realized it was me.

"We need to talk," I said as I held on to his handshake.

He gave me a campaign smile. "Yes. Yes. I'm glad you're here."

Tim Reed was nearby. Danner summoned him over with a finger.

"Tim, take Mr. Pool to the campaign bus." To me he said, "I'll see you there as soon as I can. Just hold tight."

Tim Reed led me around to the other side of the Capitol to the coach bus that served as Danner's traveling campaign headquarters. We went in.

At the rear, seats had been removed to accommodate an office and conference room, with a couch, padded swivel chairs, tables, telephones and other electronic equipment. Reed set a paper cup of coffee in front of me and sat.

"Why don't you tell me what this urgent business is," he said. "Maybe we can save the candidate some time."

"I don't want to be difficult, but as I said on the phone, this is for his ears only, or at least his ears first."

That appeared not to set well with Reed, but he didn't have much choice in the matter.

Paul Danner showed up after about fifteen minutes, escorted by some other members of his retinue. He came back and joined Reed and me at the table.

He said, "Mr. Pool, I want to thank you for whatever role you might have played in the return of my son." He spoke with a kind of facile bluster, as if still in campaign mode, and I had the feeling he was trying to establish that we had no more business to conduct.

"Have you seen him?" I said.

"Not yet, but we've been in touch by phone. I trust that the $10,000 we gave you proved sufficient."

"We're getting ahead of ourselves," I said. "There are some things you need to know. As far as I'm concerned, I'm still on the case."

His smile became fixed, and his eyes betrayed puzzlement combined with wariness.

"What things?"

"I had it in mind to tell you this privately."

"Tim has my complete confidence and trust."

Reed got up and drew a curtain across the width of the bus to separate us from the others.

"When I talked to you in Rhinelander, I said I wasn't certain what the Nazis had in mind for Eric. Now I have a pretty good idea."

Reed interrupted. "Is your idea based on what you heard from that questionable source of yours?"

"I'm working on the assumption that what she told me was true, and you'd be well advised to hear what I have to say."

Paul Danner sat back on his swivel chair, crossed one leg over the other, and with an indulgent smile said, "Let's hear what you have to say."

Tim Reed checked his watch.

I said, "If you've kept up with the news, you know that soon before we met in Rhinelander, a young guy shot up the parking lot of the Indian casino on the Lac du Flambeau reservation up there. He got away and later showed up in Wausau, where he shot some Asian immigrants. From there he went to UW Stevens Point and shot a student and a faculty member, both African Americans. The victims at the casino were white, but the hit appears to have been designed to damage the Indian interests.

The others were probably selected by race, or at least color. Outside Stevens Point the shooter was cornered by police and died in a standoff that sounds like virtual suicide. He was almost certainly sent out from the North Star compound, after getting some of the same treatment there that I told you Eric got."

"We know the story," Reed said. "But none of what we heard mentioned that the guy came from the North Star compound."

"That's because his presence there can't be traced or confirmed."

Reed said, "Let me guess: You know about the North Star connection from this so-called source of yours."

"That's right. And this is where Eric comes in. I'm convinced he's been broken, programmed and trained, and that he's been sent out to do the same kind of work and probably to expend himself in the process. I think the timing of his return to Milwaukee is tied to the coming of numerous high-profile black civil rights leaders in a few days for a rally and demonstration over the Travis Isely case. They ought to form a nice tight target."

Reed put a smirk on his face. What I said next wiped it off.

"Given your ex-wife's role in this business," I said to Paul Danner, "and her motives for wanting to hurt you, as I understand them, I also think you may be on Eric's hit list."

Reed stood. "This has gone far enough."

Danner held up a hand. Reed sat.

"What you're not accounting for," Danner said in an even tone, "is that I've talked to Eric and I'm convinced he's fine. And you might as well know that when I return to Milwaukee I'll be putting him to work for my campaign."

"Doing what?"

"He'll be a flunky," Danner said with a little laugh. "Everything from clerical stuff to working the phones to filing to manual labor—packing and unpacking, hauling boxes—whatever needs to be done that the experts don't do. There's a lot of grunt work that goes on behind the scenes of a political campaign, as you might guess. It'll be good experience for him, something to keep him occupied until school starts up again."

"He's going back to school?"

"He says he's ready to put spring semester behind him. He wants to transfer to UW, right here in Madison."

"How much did he say about his time up north?"

"I gather that he tried to come to some kind of reasonable terms with his mother, for which I don't blame him. I suspect that he knows now what I've known for a long time, that that's not possible, that she's beyond reason. As far as I'm concerned, this whole business was an attempt on her part to use him to harm me."

"That's exactly my point," I said. "And I'm convinced that the harm intended is much worse than you're willing to admit. When you first came to me you said you thought of putting Eric to work on your campaign. When he returned from up north, did he mention the idea?"

Danner looked at Reed.

Reed said, "We all agree that it's a good idea."

"I take that to mean yes."

Reed said, "It seems to me that we're at an impasse. You profess to believe something is in the works that we're convinced isn't possible. I think I'm speaking for the candidate in pointing out that you were hired to find Eric and to bring him back." Danner nodded. "Well, he's back, and we believe he's fine and nowhere near the state you describe. We don't know if his return is due in whole or in part to your efforts, but clearly you expended significant time and energy on the matter. If the $10,000 you were given isn't sufficient to cover your fee and expenses, we're open to seeing an itemization and a bill for more."

"The ten-thousand will do. If anything, I may owe you a partial refund."

Reed said, "Either way, we consider the case closed and your services no longer needed."

"I'm afraid I don't," I said. "If I'm right, this goes way beyond your interests. I can't sit back and let Eric do what I think he's planning."

Paul Danner surprised me at that point. Instead of deferring to Reed to play it out to the end, instead of getting blustery, he put a confident smile on his face, stood, and said, "I'm very busy. I wish we could part on better terms, but Tim's right, the job I hired you to do is finished, and you've been paid. We have nothing more to talk about. But I have to warn you that if you go about casting aspersions on my son's character and intentions, we could end up against each other in court. Neither of us wants that. It would be embarrassing and distracting, harmful to my interests and yours."

"Is that a threat?"

"It's a clear statement of how things stand. You'll excuse us now. We have a campaign to run."

They stood and waited for me to make as graceful a departure as I could. Seeing no other option, I did.

CHAPTER 19

I felt like I needed to sleep more than I needed to breathe, but I was driven on by a sense of urgency. On my way back to Milwaukee I called Nancy Kane on my cell phone. She said I could come to her apartment. I got there around six o'clock.

Her sweet, fresh face and voice and demeanor were a fine antidote to all I had seen and done since I had gone north. This time, I accepted her offer of a glass of apple juice.

"What can you tell me?" I said.

"All I know is, Eric's back. He got back a couple days ago. I've seen him come and go a few times and heard him next door, but we haven't run into each other and I haven't talked to him. I've been busy and haven't been around a lot. You don't look so good."

"Assault and battery and lack of sleep will do that to a guy. I'll explain another time. Is he there now?"

"I'm not sure. Care to tell me what this is all about?"

"What I know is that Eric has spent the past few weeks in far northern Wisconsin with his biological mother on a white supremacist compound. What I believe is that he returned programmed for assassination. The guy who went on a shooting rampage up north a few days ago was sent out by the same people that worked on Eric, and Eric's return right before that rally and march next week gives me a bad feeling. I think there's even a chance that his father is in the crosshairs."

"Have you told anyone else about this?" Nancy said.

"I told his dad earlier today over in Madison, but he's not buying it. At least he says he's not. Eric got in touch with him to let him know he's back. Based on a phone conversation, he believes, or pretends to, that Eric's fine. But he hasn't seen him yet."

Nancy sat quietly, absorbing it all with a kind of deer-in-the-headlights look.

"You may be able to help," I said.

"How?"

"All I'm asking is that you keep your eyes and ears open and let me know of any developments with Eric."

"I can do that, but not until Monday. I'm going up to Appleton for a family reunion—leaving tomorrow and coming back Sunday night."

"Okay. I'm especially interested to know if the other guy shows up again. His name is Brad Schale, and you were right to be creeped out by him. He's bad news. But don't stick your neck out."

"I won't."

A young man passed in front of Nancy's front window on the way to the next apartment.

For all Eric Danner had been the focus of my existence for the past few weeks, I had yet to lay eyes on him, but I was fairly certain it was him.

"Speak of the devil?" I said.

Nancy nodded.

"If I went next door to talk to him right now, he might pick up on my coming directly from here. Would that make you feel compromised?"

"I don't think he noticed us through the window just now. Anyway, Eric wouldn't hurt me. If it was the other guy I'd feel different. You might as well know, by the way, that I have trouble seeing Eric doing what you say you think he might, especially to his own dad."

"What do you base that on?"

"Call it woman's intuition."

"I thought that went out with women's lib."

She made a face and shook her head. "Don't believe it. I don't doubt that you have good reason to think what you think, but I see something in Eric that would override any brainwashing. Sensitivity, conscience, whatever you want to call it. I just can't see him as a killer."

"And maybe you bring out the best in him because you have charms to soothe the savage breast."

"I thought it was beast."

"I'm going next door. Wish me luck."

"I'll pray for you instead."

CHAPTER 20

As quietly and unobtrusively as I could, I exited Nancy's apartment and went next door and knocked. Eric opened the door on a chain and stood behind the crack. Not knowing what his state of mind was at that moment, I didn't know what approach to take. I went for a straightforward one.

I said, "My name's Barry Pool, Eric. I work for your father, and I'd like to talk to you."

"Are you with the campaign?"

"No."

"What's this about, then?"

He seemed skittish and wired, which I actually preferred to his being calm and centered, in that I'd have a better chance of getting him to reveal something in an unguarded moment.

"It's about your time up north. I'll be honest with you. I'm a private detective, and your dad hired me to find you when you disappeared. He was worried about you."

"I never disappeared. I was always visible." He gave out a nervous, humorless laugh. "People in science fiction stories disappear. Poof." He waved a hand. "Then they reappear somewhere and don't know where they are. I always knew."

"Can I come in so we can talk?"

"What's to talk about? You were hired 'cause I was missing—although I never was—and here I am."

But he didn't shut the door.

"Maybe we could talk out here. If you want, we can go somewhere. I'll buy you a cup of coffee."

He closed the door, unchained it, and came out. He faced me along the railing and spread his arms.

"Here I am. Talk."

"Your dad was concerned over the time you spent up north and how you spent it. I would be too if I was him, given the company you were in."

"I was with my mother. We had fences to mend. My dad knows that."

"Did you mend those fences?"

"That's none of your business."

"Look, Eric, I'm not out to get you, but I faced considerable risk and spent considerable time and energy focused on you and your welfare, and I need some closure, some assurances."

"Assurances of what?"

I didn't yet want to express my full suspicions about what he was up to lest I lose him before learning more.

"That during your time up north you weren't damaged by your mom and Brad Schale."

He was suddenly his mother's son. His eyes squirmed and shifted, as if in search of an escape route. But he didn't move from the spot.

"I don't know anybody by that name," he said.

"Sure you do. He's your mom's stepson. He spent time in this apartment before you left. He took you north. I think he has his hooks in you."

"Get out," he said, as if we were inside his place. "I don't have to listen to this. If you come back I'll charge you with harassment or stalking or something."

I thought it best to back off. Whether or not my theory about his intentions was on target, I'd seen enough to convince me that Eric Danner was walking along a thin edge, and I didn't want to push him over it.

I stepped past him and went down the gallery, avoiding any glance through Nancy Kanes's window as I passed it, in case Eric was watching. I heard his door slam behind me. I went to my car and drove off, on a sleepless, strung-out edge of my own.

I drove to my apartment and, without first undressing or showering or brushing my teeth, fell onto my bed and into sweet oblivion until mid-morning the next day.

CHAPTER 21

That next day was Saturday, and I awoke to it with the vague remembrance of having dreamed that, somehow, Jill and Lisa Moody and Nancy Kane had morphed into one woman who alternated between being a seductive tramp and primly chaste, leaving me uncertain and off balance. Beyond that, to my relief, I could recall no narrative thread.

With Nancy Kane gone for the weekend, I decided to keep an eye on Eric's apartment. I spent most of the rest of the day and evening staked out on the street, from where I could see Eric's SUV and his front door. On Saturday night his light was on, but other than that he didn't leave or have visitors.

I returned the next day after early morning mass, breaking my rule against working on Sunday. Around five-thirty Brad Schale came in a gray Buick. I wasn't surprised; it made sense that he wouldn't trust Eric Danner to stay on task without supervision. Maybe, too, he brought along a dose of chemical courage for Eric. He parked on the street and went up to Eric's apartment and appeared to let himself in with his own key.

After only a few minutes Schale and Eric Danner came out. They got into Schale's car and drove off. I got behind them.

They made their way to I-94, took it south, exited at Layton Avenue and headed east into Cudahy. At Packard Avenue they turned into a residential neighborhood. They parked on a narrow north-south street lined with neat bungalows behind tiny front yards. I watched from the end of the street. They got out and went into a house in the middle of the block. I drove slowly down.

A few of the houses had someone out front, either tending to flowers or sitting on the porch digesting kielbasa and cabbage, or so my stereotyping imagination led me to think. I was an outsider, and I was being monitored. A few open parking spaces were available, but sitting on a stakeout in full view of the neighborhood watch was out of the question. I stopped in front of the house Schale and Eric had gone into and wrote down the house number and the license number of a car in the driveway. At the house next door a middle-aged guy in a white tank undershirt stood on high alert on his front porch.

I turned off the block, but I wasn't out of the neighborhood yet. The ride back to the interstate took me through more narrow streets. I was watched the whole way.

I drove home and called Jill. I wasn't yet ready to see her and deal with her, but I needed her help. She said I could catch her the next morning, briefly, on her way to an assignment. I gave her the number of the house in Cudahy and the license plate number of the car in the driveway and asked if she'd be a dear and run those for me and maybe have something when we met.

She supposed she could. I offered as usual to pay for her services. She declined as usual because it pleased her to have me in her debt.

We met the next morning for coffee at George Webb's near the *Journal Sentinel* building. She had the information for me, but let me dangle a while before handing it over.

"What's this about?" she said.

Omitting the details, I gave her a brief rundown of my time up north and told her of what I suspected was afoot.

She shook her head, skepticism on her face. "I think your imagination is working overtime. That happens to men who go too long without a woman."

The words were no sooner out of her mouth than I could see that she realized she had made too hasty an assumption about my conduct up north, and that she could see that I could see that she realized it. It was *my* turn to let *her* dangle. I smiled enigmatically and allowed the awkwardness to be all hers. I enjoyed the moment immensely, then substituted warmth for enigma in my smile and said, "It has been a long time. But who's to say how long is too long?"

She gave me a sardonic look and pulled some sheets of paper from her briefcase and handed them to me across the table.

We spoke vaguely of getting together for dinner "or whatever"—her words, delivered with a flippancy that indicated an end to the conversation and my dismissal—but didn't set a date. I left and went to my office to look at what Jill had dug up.

The car in the driveway was registered to Doug Eicken, twenty-seven years old, of the address in Cudahy. His father, Darryl Eicken, age fifty-two, was in prison on a racketeering charge stemming from his days with a motorcycle gang that had been waging a protracted turf war with another gang in southern

Wisconsin and northern Illinois. What I knew that wasn't on Jill's report was that both gangs were on the fringe of the white supremacist movement, but had fallen out over traffic in drugs, weapons, and prostitutes.

The house in Cudahy belonged to Gladys Eicken, mother of Darryl, grandmother to Doug. She was seventy-seven, the widow of Karl Eicken, who had died a few years after retiring from his job as a machinist at a steel and wire factory in South Milwaukee. My guess was that Doug Eicken was living with his grandmother and using her house as a meeting place and staging ground without her knowledge.

Jill, whose patience and talent for research exceeded mine by some exponential factor, had come through for me again. That was the good news. The bad news was that now I owed her.

CHAPTER 22

As an investigative journalist, I had plenty of contact with cops. Some I knocked heads with. A few became friends. Of that last group, one was Andy Matuszak, an MPD detective who never showed the distaste for journalists that some cops do. We ended up playing Y-league basketball together and double-dating to Bucks games or for dinner and a show. When I was still unsure about making the career jump, he helped convince me I could. Brad Schale's reappearance in town had nudged me toward feeling obliged to give the police a heads-up, so I called Andy, figuring he'd give me as fair a hearing as anyone among the cops. He was able to squeeze me in for a quick meeting at Delaney's early in the afternoon of the same day I met Jill.

"How's your game?" I said when our beers came.

"Half a step slower," he said. "Still good enough to school you. What's this serious matter on your mind?"

"Do you want the short version or the long one?"

"I want one beer's worth. I'm on duty, and that's one more than my limit, but I'm willing to break the rules for a friend."

In brief, I told him about the case, where and how I had spent the past couple of weeks, what I had seen and heard, what I thought was going down, and Brad Schale's return to town and the Cudahy angle.

I said, "I'm assuming Eric Danner's mindset will more or less match that of the shooter up north, the only difference being the dynamics of the mission. I believe there's a good chance he'll be in possession of serious firepower and have a nice tight cluster of targets to use it on."

Andy said, "What have you got that justifies a warrant for a search or an arrest?"

"No more than what I just told you."

"That would be a problem in the best of times, but one we could maybe get around. As the department stands right now, there's no way you'll get anyone to move on this, including me. Nobody's willing to go outside the book or take initiative on anything."

"Because of the chief?"

He shook his head and pulled one corner of his mouth to the side.

"King Cedric, His Paranoid Majesty, is consumed by the haunting fear that something in *his* department might happen that he doesn't have absolute control over. I don't know if you're up to date on this, and even if you are, there's plenty stirring below the surface. We've got about fifteen hundred officers and over a thousand internal investigations going on.

"I know you well enough to know you're not hallucinating, Barry, but I need something more solid before I stick my neck out by moving against your suspect, especially when you factor in the political complications his dad creates. By the way, I'm on a multi-agency task force working on meth, and Brad Schale is on our watch list."

"I'm not surprised. My source up north said the soldiers being trained by North Star are getting jacked on meth, and he may be their source for the stuff. I know he's the one pulling Eric Danner's strings."

Andy said, "I'll be honest, if you're wanting to take Schale down, or asking me to, we may have a conflict. At least for now, we're letting him do his thing in the hope that he'll lead us to bigger fish."

"My main concern right now is Eric Danner. Can I at least talk you into showing up at that rally on Wednesday?"

"Maybe. I've got a task force meeting coming up in Kenosha, date to be set. If I'm in town and free, I'll consider it. Either way, you can bet there'll be lots of blue on the scene. You're shaking your head."

"That's right. I know I'm not giving you much, and I can accept what you say about the department and the chief. And yet . . ."

"And yet this bloody awful thing might happen, even though we can see it coming, even though it looks like we should be able to do something about it."

"Yeah."

"I see it all the time."

"But in this case the names of the targets are big and recognizable."

"It's a difference of degree, not of kind. I'm sorry, Barry, but I can't help you unless and until you come up with something more solid."

"Do you believe me?"

"I believe you believe it. I know I hope you're wrong."

He raised his glass, tipped it back and drained it, then stood.

"Thanks for the beer," he said.

"How do you figure?"

"You called the meeting."

CHAPTER 23

From what I had seen of Karen Danner in my office, I wasn't looking forward to approaching her, but my time and options were limited, and I thought if anyone could move Paul Danner from one line of thinking to another it was her. Whether I could convince her of the need to do so was another matter. I knew she wasn't traveling with her husband's campaign. After my meeting with Andy I decided to see if I might catch her at home.

The Danner house in Brookfield was one of those places a real estate agent trying to sell it would call *stately*—a brick, two-story Georgian with ivy growing up the walls and surrounded by broad expanses of professionally landscaped grounds. It was on a cul-de-sac, backed by woods, in the Vincent Park neighborhood, which that same agent would call *prestigious*. I parked at the curb and walked up to the front door and rang the doorbell.

The door opened on a fetching young black woman in a

maid's uniform, complete with apron and cap. I told her my name and that I worked for Mr. Danner, counting on her not knowing that that was no longer true, and told her I needed to speak with Mrs. Danner on urgent business. Before she could respond, Karen Danner appeared behind her.

"Welcome, Mr. Pool," she said.

The maid opened the door all the way and stood aside. I went in. Karen Danner gave me a sincere smile and a firm handshake.

"I'm afraid Paul's not here," she said. "Can I help you?"

"It's you I came to talk to."

"That's fine. Let's talk in my favorite spot in the house."

She led me to a sunny room with lots of plants, books, and soft leather seating. The outside wall was mostly glass, with a door that led to a backyard garden where a silver-haired gentleman tended to flowers. At her invitation, I sat. She sat across from me.

She was simply, expensively, and tastefully dressed in sandals, beige linen shorts and a green, sleeveless silk top that went nicely with the plants. She wore dangly earrings in copper and jade and a matching necklace. Her black hair, with subtle streaks of gray, was tied back casually. She was tan and looked fit, and when she crossed her fine legs I'm sure I didn't do a very good job of hiding my appreciation of her. If she noticed, and I believe she did, she seemed not to mind.

The maid had followed us and stood waiting.

"Lemonade, please, Victoria," Karen Danner said.

I'd have preferred coffee, but she didn't ask.

Victoria left. Karen Danner leaned forward and clasped her hands in front of the knee of her top leg.

"What's on your mind, Mr. Pool?"

"Eric. I have reason to believe he's planning to commit

murder, and that your husband might be one of his intended victims. Did you know he was back?"

Her composure was unflinching.

"Yes, I know. What makes you think such awful things?"

"What I saw and heard up north when I went there looking for him. I won't go into detail, but I think his will has been broken and that he's been sent out as an assassin, that he's poised to strike at that rally and march in downtown Milwaukee in a couple of days."

"Have you spoken with Paul about this?"

"Yes. He dismisses the idea. I've come here hoping you might be able talk sense into him. There's a lot at stake in this."

"If you're right."

Victoria brought a tray with a glass pitcher and tumblers of ice. She set it down and poured then left. The lemonade tasted fresh-squeezed.

Karen Danner said, "I'm afraid Paul and I are barely in touch while he's traveling around the state. And to be frank, the lines of communication between us aren't in good repair at the moment. This whole thing with Eric has been a strain, of course. So has the campaign. For a while I tried to have a say in things, but I got pushed out by Tim Reed. He made it clear that he couldn't do his job with me around. He's very strong willed and controlling." She smiled. "Like me. I admit it. That was the problem. I stepped aside to save Paul from having to make a difficult choice. I value his winning more than having a say in how he wins."

"What choice do you think he would have made?"

"That's beside the point. I declined to force the issue because I didn't want to cause damage. I pick my battles carefully, and that one wasn't worth fighting."

"You don't sound terribly concerned about what I've just told you."

"You mistake me, then. It's just that I'm a realist when it comes to the limits of what people can accomplish. And I don't spend time straining against those limits."

She seemed sincere, and she had taken me into her confidence more than I'd have expected. In fact, her manner was entirely different from what it had been in my office with her husband—warmer and less imperious. Along with her splendid good looks, the effect was disarming.

Her good looks hadn't escaped me then, but sitting across from me in her sunny library, she struck me as a first-rate beauty—sophisticated, mature, Levantine. For those needing a comparison, Anne Bancroft will do nicely. I indulged in a brief fantasy in which her next move was to assure me of the servants' discretion and invite me upstairs for a tumble. If she had, unlike with Jill or with Lisa Moody, I might very well have chucked my code of conduct and had a go of it. One for the confessional.

She said, "There is something you might be interested to know. Eric has been here."

"When?"

"Last night. He needed money. He has an allowance for certain amounts at certain intervals, and when Paul is gone it's up to me to see that he gets it. I gave him some within that allowance."

"A check?"

"He wanted cash. I got it out of the safe."

"I hope I'm not out of line in asking how much."

"Five-hundred dollars."

"No questions asked?"

"It's not for me to question. I acted according to Paul's instructions."

"How did Eric seem to you?"

"Not homicidal, although odd and skittish. But that's Eric. In this case, though, I attributed it in part to the friend that was with him." A look of distaste came to her face. "He managed to be crude and unpleasant without saying a word."

"Did he come in with Eric?"

"Yes. Eric introduced him simply as Brad. I wanted him to stay in the foyer, but I didn't quite know how to say so. He came all the way in and stood and looked around while I dealt with Eric. Eric seemed nervous about having him with him here in the house. *I* certainly was."

"That was Brad Schale, Frieda Schale's stepson. I met him up north. He's bad news."

"I guessed that. As they left, he was out the door first. I caught Eric for a moment and told him discreetly that I didn't want him bringing him back here."

"What did he say?"

"He didn't say anything. He looked helpless and a little frightened, like he might not be able to do anything about it."

CHAPTER 24

I got on I-94 in Brookfield and headed into town. I hadn't decided if I would go home or to my office, but figured either way I might benefit from a drive along the lake with my windows down.

At the entrance to 794 a set of twin billboards next to the highway caught my eye. Both had oversized head shots—one of LeRoy Givens, complete with dreadlocks and stoned eyes and a pitch for his radio talk show; the other of Terrell Robinson, whose *Journal Sentinel* column made him, according to the text on the sign, "Black Milwaukee's First Word in Journalism." I knew Terrell well enough to know that he wouldn't care for the implication that he was writing exclusively for black Milwaukee. I had seen those signs plenty of times before, but in the state I was in at the moment—at a loss for what to do next or who to approach next—the one featuring Terrell suggested to me my next move.

Terrell Robinson came to the *Journal* as a beat reporter fresh out of journalism school at Northwestern about four years before I left. He quickly established a reputation at the paper and in town for being pugnacious, meticulous and thorough. And the man could *write*. After about three years he got his own column. He was iconoclastic, honest (at times to a fault, if that's possible) and a wicked satirist. His first allegiance was not to his race, but to the truth. His targets of choice were foolishness, arrogance, injustice and humbuggery. I dread the day that I might become the object of his invective.

It was around four-thirty. I decided to try catching Terrell at the *Journal Sentinel* building in the hopes of enlisting him in my cause. It was probably too late for him to run a column on what I thought was afoot, assuming he'd be inclined to, but I hoped I might convince him to spread the word through his network of connections, effectively raising the alarm. I parked on the street and entered the lobby. The receptionist was the same as when I left, Bertie Oliver.

"Barry Pool," she said. "Let me guess, the private eye biz ain't what it was cracked up to be and you're back begging for a job."

"Charming as always, Bertie. Actually, I was hoping to catch Terrell Robinson."

Bertie rang his number, waited, hung up, and was informing me that he must have left for the day when he stepped out of the lobby elevator.

"Terrell," I called out and headed his way.

He stopped. "Look who the cat drug in."

We met and shook hands. Terrell was a big, burly guy with an effusive aura of welcome about him.

"Tell me what I'm interrupting or keeping you from doing," I said.

"I'm headed for Leon's to work a source. What's on your mind?"

"Bloody awful stuff," I said. "Can you spare me ten minutes?"

He put his arm around my shoulder and practically carried me along with him as he headed for a side exit that led to a parking lot.

"Tell you what, my man, come along with me to Leon's and spill your guts. I'll work you in around my source. You'll be the palest stuff there, but you'll be with me, so have no fear."

Outside, The Oak was leaning against Terrell's silver Lexus.

The Oak had spent some time at offensive tackle for the Packers until he blew out a knee, later a stretch in the pen for something or other. In recent years he freelanced around town as a bodyguard and who knew what else. If William Perry was "The Refrigerator," The Oak, with his stone-cold demeanor, was "The Upright Freezer." This wasn't the first time Terrell had hired him to keep him company until the heat was off.

"I'll take my car and meet you there," I said. "Are you going directly?"

"No stops. Be there in seven minutes, ten if there's traffic."

Terrell got in the passenger side. The Oak got behind the wheel.

Leon's was just across the river on East Wells St. The cars in the lot were all newer and much more expensive than mine. The Oak stayed outside and we went in.

The place was about half full of Milwaukee's black professional class, all of them well dressed, a good number of them decked out in gold and precious gems. Walking in with Terrell was like being with a celebrity. We didn't pass one table from which he wasn't greeted. At several he paused to shake hands and exchange a few words as we made our way to an empty booth near the back. I saw no evidence of his being in trouble with this segment of Milwaukee's black community. I was The Invisible Man.

A waiter came. Terrell ordered Jim Beam and soda on the rocks. I had Bass Pale Ale. It seemed appropriate—what Terrell told me about my being the palest stuff there turned out to be true. The drinks came.

"I feel like a bar of Ivory soap," I said.

"Ninety-nine and forty-four one-hundredths percent pure," Terrell said with a hearty laugh. "Question is, what's the other fifty-six hundredths been up to?"

"Nothing that would sell tabloids."

"Tell me what's on your mind, Barry. From the look on your face, I'm guessing big trouble."

I took a pull on my ale.

"Junius Cato, David Sojourner, the Reverend Starr. If I'm right, they're all targets for assassination at that rally and march coming up, with a high likelihood of collateral damage."

"That's a heck of a scenario. Who's doing the assassinating?"

"Paul Danner's son."

"Where you coming from on this?"

I gave him a condensed version.

"Weapons of choice?" Terrell said.

"Whatever causes the most damage. Guns. Maybe explosives. Maybe both. I'm betting he'll be on a suicide mission and acting alone, that he'll inflict as much damage as he can until somebody stops him, with a bullet or otherwise."

"You sure you haven't been reading too much news from the Middle East?"

"I think I know how this sounds," I said. "But suppose I'm right."

"Then we've got disaster on our hands. Why come to me?"

"Everybody I've gone to with this, including Paul Danner, either isn't buying it or says they're helpless to do anything about it. I'm looking for somebody who believes me and can do something."

"What can *I* do?"

"Run this by your connections and get the word out on the street. Anything to send up the red flag."

Terrell shook his head.

"This is way too speculative. I don't want to see this happen any more than you do, but you haven't convinced me it will. If I do what you ask I could get accused of trying to undermine the rally, and things are hot enough for me already." He checked his watch. "Try Givens. He's on the air in a few minutes. You get through to him you'll be talking to a whole lot of people."

"You know how I feel about him."

"Yeah, I do. And you know what, I feel the same. He's a clown and a racist. And white people in this town should send up prayers of thanksgiving for him."

"I don't follow."

"He's a steam valve." He leaned toward me over the table and lowered his voice. "Black folks hear that crap of his on the radio and eat it up." He glanced around the room. "Maybe not the ones here, but the ones on the street with all the anger and frustration. He's their voice. He vents their rage, some of it, anyway. Take away LeRoy Givens and this town would explode."

Unprompted, the waiter came with another drink for Terrell. I passed on a second ale. Terrell stood.

"My source just came in. You want an escort to the door?"

"I can manage. Think I need one to my car?"

"If we were on the north side you might, but not here. Besides, The Oak's out there. He knows you came with me. He'll take care of you."

"I could have used The Oak up north."

"He'd've blended in real good."

Outside, The Oak was leaning against the back of Terrell's car, his meaty arms crossed over his massive chest, a picture of impassivity. I considered asking for one of his business cards, but thought better of it.

CHAPTER 25

I drove off and worked my way toward the lake. Downtown rush hour traffic was almost gridlocked. Perhaps thinking of what Terrell had said about Givens, I turned on the radio and set it to scan. Serially, I heard a firefighter sharing weird tales and strange encounters from his job; Mr. Angry ranting; smooth jazz; talk; frantic jazz; more talk; music, so-called, by a group whose name I missed but which I would have named Ugly and Hateful. The city was about to explode, or so I thought, and radio stations were fighting the ratings war.

Then I heard LeRoy Givens.

Before turning to talk radio, Givens had been a city alderman. He used both positions to wage open war on Milwaukee's white establishment, a war he wasn't shy of fighting as a front-line soldier. He incited riots then joined them. He baited the cops into coming down on him, and then charged them with brutality and racism when they did. (In a moment of frankness in a *Milwaukee Magazine* feature, he claimed to play with a full deck—"all of them race cards.") On the radio he was Rush Limbaugh in dreadlocks—arrogant and shrill, full of bombast, disdainful of truth, reason and logic.

I stopped the scan and listened. Givens's topic was the rally and march. He predicted that it would be the biggest and most meaningful public outcry for racial justice in Milwaukee's history. He named the luminaries planning to attend—not only Junius Cato and David Sojourner and the Reverend Starr, but also artists, athletes, academics, authors, local clergy. I had heard that plenty of white politicians and other public figures had also announced their intentions to be there, but his list contained only the names of blacks.

Call-in time came. Traffic was stop-and-go, but mostly stop. I got out my cell phone and punched his number, without much hope of getting through.

My first three attempts got busy signals. On the fourth I connected, not directly to Givens on the air, but to a woman screening calls. She asked me what I intended to say. I gave it to her straight, expecting her to hang up. Instead, she told me to hold and to turn down my radio.

I turned the volume to low and listened to Givens deal with a caller ahead of me, then another. Then I was on the air.

"Thanks for calling Black Milwaukee Perspectives. What's on your mind?"

I identified myself by profession only, leaving out my name, and in ever so sketchy terms, again avoiding names, explained what I thought was afoot and why I thought so.

"How would you like the outcry for racial justice you're anticipating to descend into murder and mayhem?" I said.

"My man," Givens said, "black Milwaukeeans have been suffering murder and mayhem at the hands of the police and the white power structure for a long time. Anyone who wants to take your warning seriously can stay home. But yours truly will be there, and I'll tell you why. I don't believe you. I think you're trying to sabotage the most impressive gathering of black activists and advocates this town has ever seen. I think if I didn't want that to happen, I'd do exactly what you're doing—I'd call in a bomb threat. Sorry, but it won't work. Milwaukee's gonna hear the black voice cry out for justice. Milwaukee's gonna have to listen to that voice, and no amount of threatening talk gonna silence it. Thanks for your call, Mr. Detective."

The line went dead. I was off the air.

I turned up the radio and heard Givens say, "Thanks for calling Black Milwaukee Perspectives. What's on your mind?"

I turned it off and crept through rush hour traffic toward the East Side. I felt like the poor lonely guy in the sci-fi films who knows for a fact that aliens have arrived with superior powers and hostile intentions but can't get anyone to listen, or if they do they either dismiss him as nuts or fabricate some plausible explanation for why what he saw isn't really what he thinks he saw.

CHAPTER 26

Since I couldn't get my mind off of the Eric Danner case, and since I didn't want to take work home with me, I went to my office instead of my house. The day had been as frustrating a one as I had ever spent since switching careers. I sat at my desk in a blue funk, staring at the brick wall outside my window, as if searching for clarity regarding my next move. The only thing that became clear was the silliness of this whole business of looking for answers on the brick wall outside my window, so I got up and lowered the blind. I'm not normally given to fatalism, but I was feeling fatalistic then, resigned to the fact that in spite of my best efforts the worst would happen—inevitably, inexorably—and I could do nothing about it.

There came a knocking on the door, loud and insistent. I considered not answering, but whoever it was didn't sound inclined to give up and go away. The knocks came in sets of three.

Bang! Bang! Bang! . . . Bang! Bang! Bang! Even after deciding to answer, it took me a while to overcome inertia and rise from the chair. *Bang! Bang! Bang!* By the time I got to the door, I imagined finding Macduff and Lennox on the other side.

What I found was Tim Reed, alone, looking grim and severe and accusatory. I wished I had stayed in my chair.

"We need to talk," he said.

Uninvited, he brushed past me and in. We went to my desk and sat across from each other. I didn't offer coffee or anything else.

"I'll get right to the point," he said. "We learned from Eric that you showed up at his apartment suggesting that he may be in an unbalanced mental state and up to something dangerous."

Interesting. With Eric that day outside his apartment I had been deliberately vague about my estimation of his mental state and said nothing about what I thought he was planning. In reporting to Reed and his father it seemed he might have unwittingly hinted at his intentions.

I didn't respond.

"I hope you haven't shared this harebrained theory of yours with anyone else," Reed said.

"If I did it's because I'm trying to prevent murder from happening."

"We see no potential for what you're suggesting, and we insist that you back off. You've been paid for finding and returning Eric, but we're willing to add a certain amount to that to lay this to rest. Call it a bonus."

"I'd call it a bribe. Besides, Eric's return probably had nothing to do with me. At best I flushed him. I'm convinced he came back because his programming was complete and the people that programmed him saw the rally as a good place to put it, and him, to use. In their delusional state, they think he'll be a catalyst for the launching of a holy war to save this country for the white race."

"Has it occurred to you that you're the one that's delusional?"

"Actually it has," I said. "And if I am, then I'll be hurting myself—my reputation and professional standing—more than anyone else. I'm willing to take that chance. But if Eric manages to pull off what I think he's planning, there'll be hell to pay."

Reed gave me a hard look.

"We're not getting anywhere," he said. "My offer is still on the table, at least until I walk out the door. Call it a carrot. Now here's a stick: If you persist in this, we'll drag you into court for slander and go after your license. No matter how squeaky clean you think your record is, we'll find something, and you'll be back in the newspaper business writing obituaries—if you're lucky."

He got up and went to the door. I stayed seated. He looked back at me for a moment, giving me a last chance, then walked out.

I felt confident that Reed was bluffing about my license. Even if he used thumbscrews on Father Anthony to force him to reveal the contents of my confessions, the most he'd get was lust, gluttony, greed, sloth, anger, envy and pride, and I was pretty sure none of those provided the technical grounds for having a private investigator's license revoked.

Before Tim Reed came, I had begun to entertain the idea of not showing up at the rally and letting happen what would happen. I was no less convinced that I was right and no less convinced that I might be able to make a difference if I was there, maybe by spotting Eric Danner and disarming him before he could do serious damage. But I was frustrated and close to no longer caring. It was a cynical calculation—nihilistic, even—and

I couldn't have defended it in a court of ethics.

I had all but decided when the phone rang. I let it ring until Nancy Kane's voice came over the answering machine. I picked it up.

"Hi. Let me guess. You've decided I'm being paranoid over Eric Danner and I need professional help."

"I'm calling to let you know the creepy guy is back. What's wrong with *you*?"

"Sorry. I know he's back. Are you wanting to get out of there?"

"I'm okay with it for now. He hasn't been around much. He just showed up a couple times then took off again. Sometimes Eric went with him. Will I see you at the rally?"

I stalled. "What's your interest in it?"

"I'm doing a research project on race relations in Milwaukee for the sociology class I'm taking, and I'm hoping to get some interviews."

"Have you calculated for the risk involved if Eric is planning what I think he is?"

"I calculate for risk every time I walk out the door. Besides, who knows, if I see Eric and talk to him he might think better of what you say he's planning, assuming you're right."

"I'll look for you," I said.

CHAPTER 27

The next morning, the day before the rally and march, I went downtown to do some scouting and to try to put myself in the mind of Eric Danner, maybe make a guess at where and how he might strike.

I started at Marquette Park, where the rally was scheduled to begin at ten-thirty. I walked around and through the park, dodging panhandlers—"Can you help me?"—and looking for anything that would suggest Eric's *modus operandi*. It was all pure speculation and guesswork on my part, but I figured he'd be looking for two things to fall in place at once—the clustering of his primary targets and an opportunity to attack from up close. The likeliest time and place for that would be if and when they were together in the gazebo next to the river to deliver speeches.

From there I walked to Red Arrow Park, across from City

Hall, along the march route on the fliers that had been appearing around town. If Eric hadn't already struck in Marquette Park, he might do so at any of a number of times and places, depending on how the targets were grouped and on his tolerance for collateral damage. By the time I got back to my car I had decided that there were too many variables for me to guess what Eric would do, or when or where he'd do it. But I doubted that Eric would know in advance either. Most likely he'd show up armed as much as possible without giving himself away and look for the best opportunity to do the most damage.

There was one more thing before I left downtown. Remembering the hit on the casino up north, it had occurred to me that a similar hit on the Menominee Casino on Canal Street, by someone other than Eric just before the start of the rally, would be a good way to divert police resources away from the primary target. But in scrambling to alert people to my suspicions about Eric, I hadn't done anything about it. Not that I could, but I was curious about security there.

The casino parking lot held only a few cars, and no security was visible as I walked to the entrance. I might have appeared on a monitor somewhere, but that wouldn't have prevented me from picking off the few people coming and going on the lot. As far as I could tell, I didn't pass through a metal detector or any other device to check me for weapons when I entered.

Inside, I meandered among the slot machines and tables, as if looking for some action. I approached two guys standing together talking. They wore dark suits with name tags. One turned to me with a welcoming, helpful look on his face. His name tag said he was Tom Panetta.

"How can I help you, sir?" he said. The other guy walked off.

I said, "I'm doing research on casino security in light of

the attack that took place on the Pot O' Gold casino up north last week."

His smile shifted from sincere to official.

"I'm afraid we have a policy against discussing such matters with the public. I can assure you, though, that our security is adequate."

"Can you at least tell me if you took any extra measures after the attack up there, and if you did, whether or not those measures are still in place?"

"I'm sorry, sir, but I can't discuss that except to say that we took the issue seriously and addressed it accordingly, and that we're always extremely vigilant."

"On my way in just now, I could have done to the people in the parking lot what the guy did at the Pot o' Gold."

Panetta's countenance shifted again, as if he took what I said as a threat.

"Maybe you should be talking to our manager."

He swept his jacket back and pulled a walkie-talkie from his belt and spoke into it. A guy in a dark blue suit came through a door across the room and came our way. He was thin and dark and intense. He was also a head shorter than me and seemed to resent it.

"What's going on?" he said to Panetta, grazing me with a look as he spoke.

Panetta gave him a reasonably accurate representation of what I had said.

"The security of our customers is of the highest priority," the manager said, "Our precautions are more than adequate."

It was boilerplate, delivered in a measured, hostile tone, and left me with the impression that I got on the streets of Deering—that the bottom line trumped all other considerations.

Accumulated frustration rose up in me and took hold of my tongue.

I said, "On my way in from the parking lot just now, and after I got inside, I could have shot the place up. When I was done, would you issue a PR statement to the effect that the security of your customers is of the highest priority and that your precautions are more than adequate?"

A guy at the nearest blackjack table heard me and looked over.

I said, "The truth is, you're calculating that if that happened you'd take a hit in the short run, but that things would eventually return to normal and you'd chalk it all up to the cost of doing business."

With a high-pitched whistle and a waggle of the index finger of his right hand, the manager summoned a thuggish-looking guy with short, spiked, blond hair and a shirt open at the collar under a sport coat—a sort of white version of The Oak.

"Jerry, this gentleman needs a demonstration of the effectiveness of our security. I want you to accompany him out the door and all the way to his car. And make sure you see him drive off the parking lot."

Jerry took me by an elbow. I tried to pull free, but he tightened his grip until it hurt, a lot. He pulled me along so fast that he almost lifted me off my feet. When we got outside, he stopped.

"Which car is yours?" he said.

I pointed with my free hand.

"I can make it from here," I said.

But Jerry had his orders. He dragged me all the way to my car and released me with a hard shove that sent me into the driver's side door. I got in and rubbed and flexed my arm to see if it still worked. Jerry stood by and watched as I drove away with a new condition for the medical books: security elbow.

CHAPTER 28

That night I vacillated between self-doubt and certainty over what I had been going around saying about Eric Danner's intentions. I went to bed around midnight, anticipating fitful sleep, but slept fairly well and awoke at seven o'clock to a spattering sound on my window. I got up and looked out.

Rain fell steadily but not hard, and from the look of the sky would persist throughout the day. I brewed a pot of coffee and showered. The shower washed away some of the doubts of the night before. A mug of coffee pretty much took care of the rest.

Plenty of time remained before the start of the rally at ten-thirty. I read the newspaper, finished the pot of coffee, paced and fidgeted, looked out my window at the rain. In all my speculations about this day, I hadn't anticipated rain and how it might affect the outcome.

For one thing, it gave me a pretext to wear a hooded slicker, which made it easier to conceal both myself and my guns—the .38 in a shoulder holster and the Browning in a flap pocket. Of course Eric Danner could more easily conceal and carry the same way. Around nine o'clock I drove downtown.

I parked in a pay lot east of the Milwaukee River so that my car would be on the side of the river that the march ended on. To leave my hands free I didn't carry an umbrella, thinking that the hood of my jacket and the bill of my Brewers cap would keep me as dry as I needed to be. I crossed the river on the Wells Street bridge and went up Plankinton Avenue to Marquette Park.

Some workers were setting up a sound system on the gazebo. I walked around, then took up a position on a bench at the top of the slope at the west edge of the park for the view it afforded. The rain persisted in a light, steady drizzle. People drifted in, some with posters on sticks, many of them under umbrellas, making it hard to tell who was who. If the turnout lived up to the hype of the organizers, Marquette Park would be filled to overflowing. By ten-thirty it was less than half full. About a dozen cops in uniforms under raincoats stood in a loose perimeter well back from the crowd.

A local guy from an inner-city Baptist church got up to start the proceedings. After brief remarks and a prayer he introduced David Sojourner, who emerged from a group near the gazebo, shaking hands on the way to the microphone. Just as he started to speak, Junius Cato arrived like royalty in a caravan of three black limousines. They parked illegally, and he got out of the middle one, stepping under an umbrella held by a member of his entourage.

Like Sojourner, Cato was based in Chicago, and they both conveyed the sense that any trip they made to Milwaukee was an act of condescension, Sojourner going so far on one such occasion as to refer to Milwaukee as "Chicago Lite." They were known to be rivals, more for a place in the spotlight than for representing different spiritual traditions. Cato's people formed a cordon around him. They were dressed more or less alike, and like their leader—nattily, with trench coats over suits, white shirts and bow ties. Cato waved left and right as he progressed toward the gazebo. Actually *waved* isn't quite the word; it was more like he conferred blessings.

David Sojourner, a strained, deferential smile on his face, waited for Cato's party to reach the gazebo. When it did, Cato called out, "*Speak,* brother," as if granting permission.

David Sojourner spoke. He pointed across the park to the Milwaukee County Historical Center and remarked on the shameful history of the treatment of minorities in Milwaukee and lamented that, unfortunately, that treatment wasn't relegated to history, that it was still going on. The sound system was acting up, but I thought I heard reference to the "brutality mentality." He went on in that vein for half an hour, rhyming and waxing rhythmic, then yielded the microphone for brief remarks by the leader of a local civic organization.

I took it all in with my usual ambivalence. I have little tolerance for bluster and bombast, none at all when they threaten to unseat logic and reason. Yet whenever I grow dismissive at hearing one such as David Sojourner, I can never quite silence a voice in my head that accuses me of racism. Terrell Robinson likes to refer to the "sludge in the crankcase" that all of us, including him, have to deal with when it comes to race, no matter how enlightened we think we might be. As I sat there listening to David Sojourner, and anticipating what I'd hear from Junius Cato and the Reverend Starr, I took refuge in Terrell's metaphor.

Not that it cleared away my ambivalence, but it reminded me that I wasn't alone.

For some time I had been watching a guy standing more or less motionless near the outer edge of the crowd under an umbrella, which partially obscured his face; the part not obscured was white. His distance from the crowd and his immobility made him seem emotionally disengaged. He looked to be about Eric Danner's height and weight, but I was too far away to be certain it was him. I moved in his direction.

As I drew closer I could see that it was Eric. I got right up behind him and bear hugged him with one hand and patted him down with the other. He was clean. He turned and looked at me, eyes wide. They were bloodshot and his pupils were distended.

"It's you," Eric said to me.

"That would be a true statement even if it were someone else," I said.

"What do you think you're doing?"

"Checking for weapons."

He turned away from me and headed off to the right along the outer edge of the crowd. I followed. He stopped and faced me.

"Leave me alone."

"I'm afraid I can't do that. I came here expecting to find you. And here you are."

He ignored me, focusing his attention on the gazebo. I stayed close to him.

Junius Cato was at the microphone. Beaming and looking out at the audience as at his subjects, he warmed up with some talk of the need for love and unity, then somehow, deftly, worked his way from those to his trademark theme—the plot on the part of the devil, and his agent the white man, to eliminate the black man not only from Milwaukee but from the face of the earth. Not to be outdone by David Sojourner, Cato declaimed for thirty-five minutes, his speech punctuated by shouts of affirmation from his acolytes. All the while, Eric Danner was as immobile as if he had taken root in the soggy ground under his feet.

Some more locals had their say. The last one introduced the Reverend Marcus Starr.

Perhaps unfairly, I had always seen the Reverend Starr as more shyster than clergyman, a walking commercial for medallion necklaces and sharkskin suits. Everything about him suggested that somewhere in his home was a shrine to Sammy Davis Jr. He had first gained national attention by taking the side of the putative victims in a series of race cases that belonged more on the covers of supermarket tabloids than legitimate news outlets. But in recent years, by dint of sheer decibel level and persistence, he had managed to attract enough attention from mainstream media to pass for a legitimate public figure.

As he got up to speak, I spotted Andy Matuszak. I was reluctant to leave Eric's side, lest he sneak off and retrieve a weapon that he had stashed somewhere, but I wanted to talk to Andy, so I worked my way toward him.

"Glad you came, Andy."

"My meeting got pushed out. Still expecting trouble?"

"Yes, but maybe not here in the park. Eric Danner is here, the guy I told you about, but he's not carrying a weapon."

I turned to point out Eric, but he was gone from the spot where I had left him.

I said to Andy, "Are you marching?"

"I doubt it."

The Reverend Starr was on his peroration, which was full of

exhortation to fight for justice in our nation, and ended with the declaration that it was time to march, time to show that black Milwaukeeans—never mind that he was a black New Yorker—could "act with impact."

At that the crowd began moving out of the park, umbrellas and posters aloft, arcing around the north side of the Milwaukee County Historical Society building and onto Old World Third Street. By the time the last ones left the park—with Sojourner, Cato, and the Reverend Starr arm in arm at the head—they stretched out for a full block. Some cops accompanied on foot. Two squad cars rolled alongside in tandem.

I followed on the other side of the street, looking for Eric Danner, whom I had yet to spot after losing sight of him in Marquette Park. I didn't see him, but I saw Nancy Kane. She was working her way along the line of marchers, latching on to selected ones with a hand-held recorder.

The march went off undisturbed, with no hecklers or counter-protesters along the way—and no one attacking from ambush. Panhandlers hit up the stragglers, maybe thinking that anyone willing to march for racial justice would be good for a handout.

The parade seemed to have been timed and routed to maximize exposure to the downtown lunch crowd. It crossed Wisconsin Avenue to the south side of the street, blocking traffic for several minutes, turned left and progressed toward the river in front of the Shops of Grand Avenue. Lots of people were out, despite the rain. First to last, it took about ten minutes for the entire line to cross the river on the Wisconsin Avenue bridge.

At Water Street they turned north. The plan was to pass City Hall on the right, cross Kilbourn, and regather in Red Arrow Park. I had been keeping pace across the street toward the front of the procession, watching for Eric.

Just before the leaders came to Wells Street I saw him driving east on Wells in his SUV. He slowed and watched, then moved on. By the time I got to Wells he was out of sight. I continued on foot and entered Red Arrow Park with the first of the marchers. The rest came in over the next several minutes.

The crowd that hadn't filled Marquette Park nearly filled Red Arrow, which was smaller by half. Sojourner, Cato and the Reverend Starr stood at the south edge, across the street from City Hall. Someone produced a bullhorn. David Sojourner took it and, facing City Hall, spoke into it:

"Can you see us, Mr. Mayor? Do you know we're here? We're almost forty percent of the population of Milwaukee."

What followed was a condensed version of his spiel in Marquette Park. (Shame on me, but before he finished, I came up with a new meaning for the *bull* in bullhorn.) As he and Junius Cato and the Reverend Starr and some others took turns, I crisscrossed the crowd several times, north to south and east to west, looking for Eric Danner.

I had just got back up to the front, to the right of the speakers, when I saw him. He was alone in his SUV, going west on Kilbourn. As he came even with the park he slowed. Traffic was steady but not dense. He was in the lane nearest the park, but on the far side of his vehicle, so that his view, and any shots he might fire, would be through the passenger side window. I watched him as he rolled slowly by and looked to his right at the crowd. He was holding up traffic, and a car went around him with a horn blast. Then he was gone. I sensed he'd been doing reconnaissance, and watched for him to reappear. A couple of minutes later he did.

This time he drove east on Kilbourn. He was on the side

of the vehicle nearest the park, but with westbound traffic in between that would potentially interfere with his line of fire. But again he only slowed as he passed, peering through his open window.

How to account for my standing there in silence, more or less convinced that Eric would aim deadly fire from medium range at a dense crowd, without shouting some kind of warning to the others? I suppose I feared embarrassment if I did and was wrong.

I was certain that, having scouted from both directions, he'd come by again for a third pass and make whatever move he was planning.

And here he came, heading east again. This time he slowed to a crawl then stopped. His left hand came out of the window with a pistol in it.

It was one of those moments when the whole world seems to come to a silent halt. Whoever had been speaking saw him and stopped in mid-sentence, dropped the bullhorn and went down. For the moment, there was no traffic around Eric's SUV, giving him a clear shot. Someone near the front of the crowd pointed and yelled a warning. Those nearest the street went down or scrambled for cover. Owing in part to the proliferation of umbrellas and in part to the high emotional voltage already present, understanding of what was afoot was slow to ripple back through the crowd.

I watched, unaccountably still standing. I can't say I didn't feel fear. Certainly I didn't stand there out of bravery. I think what I felt most was curiosity, probably because all my speculation and guesswork was culminating in this moment. Had Eric Danner been inclined to, and had he been a good enough marksman, he could have shot me dead where I stood, only a few feet from him. (And Junius Cato too, who, with perhaps the courage of his convictions, stood his ground and stared straight at Eric.)

Instead, after what appeared to be a moment of indecision, Eric pointed the gun straight up and, barely above a conversational voice and entirely without enthusiasm, said, "Um, white power," fired three times, and sped off.

CHAPTER 29

Confusion and panic reigned. People screamed and scrambled every which way. After a minute, those in front nearest the action got up and looked around at each other as if for assurance that they were still alive.

The two squad cars on the scene went in hot pursuit of Eric. The cops on foot took off running after him in the same general direction. Most of those in the park who hadn't already fled now left in a semi-orderly hurry, maybe thinking that Eric might come back and do worse.

Eric had turned south on Broadway. I ran across Kilbourn and went south on Water Street, following the cops on foot ahead of me. One used a device to communicate as he ran, so I hoped he'd lead me to wherever the cops managed to catch Eric or cut him off—if they were able to.

We crossed Wells, then Mason. I was close to being out of

gas, but so were the cops, and I managed to keep up with them. I heard multiple sirens, but the buildings downtown might have been distorting the sound, so I wasn't sure where they were coming from or how far off they were. The cops turned right at Wisconsin Avenue. After doing the same I could see traffic stacked up. I headed that way.

Squad cars blocked the east side of the Wisconsin Avenue bridge. I had been running for only about ten minutes, but the cops had already formed a security perimeter. I worked my way through the crowd that had gathered until I could see Eric's SUV sitting in the middle of the street, just short of the bridge, with the driver's side door open. As I approached I expected to see him in it, slumped over the wheel, dead.

It was empty.

"Where is he?" I said to the first cop I came to.

He pointed down the River Walk running south from Wisconsin Avenue. Eric was climbing the front of construction scaffolding set up there for renovation work. It went all the way to the top, about ten stories, and blocked the River Walk between the building and the railing above the river.

"We cut him off here at the bridge," the cop said. "Down the River Walk was the only way he could go, but the scaffolding was there, so he started climbing."

I asked him where the renovators were.

He shrugged. "We didn't see any. They must not've worked today 'cause of the rain."

As he climbed, Eric slipped a couple of times on the wet metal tubing, but managed to hang on. About seven stories up, he gave out and stopped. He turned to face the river, his arms hooked behind him on a horizontal bar. He looked like a figurehead on the prow of a ship. Some cops approached the bottom of the scaffolding.

"I'll jump if you come up," Eric yelled. The cops held back.

At least for the moment it was a standoff.

"Who's in charge here?" I asked the cop.

He pointed to Captain Pat Dunleavy, with whom I had had some dealings, as both journalist and private investigator. Using a bullhorn, he ordered Eric to come down. I showed my license to the cop I had been talking with and told him about my connection to the case.

"I know Dunleavy," I said. "Can you let me in?"

He thought about it for a moment then escorted me to Dunleavy's side. Dunleavy turned to us with annoyance and impatience on his face.

"Pool," he said before the cop could explain. "Andy Matuszak told me you warned him about this. Is this the guy?"

"That's him. Do you know if he's still armed?"

"We found a gun in his vehicle. To be safe we have to assume he has another. I have a sharpshooter getting into position."

I said, "I understand that you have to work on that assumption, but I hope your man isn't trigger happy."

Dunleavy didn't appreciate that.

"He's a trained officer and as trigger happy as he needs to be to protect the public. You're going to have to sit this one out on the sidelines."

He turned away and raised his bullhorn and yelled up to Eric. "Nobody's been hurt. If it stays that way and you come down now, things will go easier on you."

Eric didn't respond.

Nothing changed for another ten minutes. I stayed close to Dunleavy. At the security perimeter, Nancy Kane was talking to the cop that I had talked to earlier. I went to them.

"She knows the guy up there," I said to the cop.

The cop shrugged. I took Nancy to Dunleavy, who was flushed with anger and frustration. I introduced them.

"I may be able to help," she said.

He gave her an incredulous look. For a minute I thought he was going to laugh.

"What can you do that we can't?" Dunleavy said, but already I could see him soften in her presence.

Nancy said, "We're friends. I think he'll listen to me. At least let me try."

Dunleavy said, "Girl, if there's one thing this kid needs right now it's a friend. But you're not authorized to make any deals. And I won't let you put yourself at risk."

"Eric won't hurt me," Nancy said. "Can I use the bullhorn?"

Dunleavy handed it to her.

"How do you work this thing?"

"It's turned on. Just point it at him and speak into it."

Nancy leaned back and spoke up into the mouthpiece.

"Eric, it's me, Nancy."

Eric hadn't noticed her arrival on the scene. When he heard her voice his head turned like the dial of a compass to magnetic north. Dunleavy watched in fascination.

"Eric, do you have your cell phone with you?"

For a second his look said "Huh?" Then he nodded.

"Can you get it out without losing your grip?"

He nodded again.

"Wait!" I yelled and waved my arms.

Dunleavy and Nancy looked at me.

"Where's your shooter?" I said to Dunleavy.

He pointed to a spot across the river where a guy dressed like a member of a SWAT team was getting into a crouch at the railing, his rifle aimed at Eric.

"He needs to know what's going on," I said. "We don't want death by misunderstanding."

As I spoke I held a hand up to Eric as a signal not to make a move.

Dunleavy spoke into a walkie-talkie. I could see the shooter listening with a device of his own. The shooter sat back on a bench and raised his gun to a vertical position. He looked like a guy in his backyard cooking steaks on the grill.

"Go ahead," Dunleavy said to Nancy.

"Okay, Eric," Nancy said through the bullhorn. "Get your cell phone out and turn it on. I'm going to call you."

Eric let go with one hand and used it to pull his phone out of a pocket of his pants. I watched the shooter. He stayed on the bench, but scooted forward at the ready. Nancy gave the bullhorn back to Dunleavy and thumbed the keypad on hers. From seventy feet below, we could hear the faint chirp of Eric's phone.

"Can I have some room?" Nancy said to me and the cops around her. "This is private."

We stepped back. She looked up at Eric and he down at her as she spoke, too quietly for us to hear. He nodded. She spoke some more. He nodded some more.

Nancy turned her phone off and put it in a pocket and smiled her sweet, cheerful smile.

"He'll be right down," she said.

We looked up. Eric had reversed himself to face the scaffolding and was on his way down.

Dunleavy looked at Nancy with surprise and a kind of deferential amazement. I looked at her the same way, minus the surprise.

The cops crowded around the spot at the bottom where Eric would set down. Nancy begged them to back off, and for a minute it looked like he wanted to climb up again when he saw them. But by then he was within reach and a cop got him by the leg and held on until he was in their midst. They cuffed him and led him off, ignoring Nancy's plea to be allowed a word with him. They took him away in a squad car.

"What did you tell him?" Dunleavy said to Nancy.

Her smile was coy.

"I gave him a reason to come down." She checked her watch. "Do you need me? I'm late for my class."

For a moment Dunleavy was speechless.

"I guess not," he finally said. "You'll hear from us later, though." Then, almost as an afterthought, "Thanks."

"No problem." She turned to me. "Later, Barry."

Her backpack slung over one shoulder, she made her way through the crowd and went bouncing west down Wisconsin Avenue, as if tripping off to Oz.

Charms to soothe the savage breast.

CHAPTER 30

I spent some time with Dunleavy to fill him in on the background and got home late in the afternoon—home instead of my office because I wanted closure.

But closure didn't come. I lay on my couch and listened to jazz on my radio, but couldn't relax. I got a bottle of ale out of my refrigerator but put it back, preferring to keep a clear head. I was too wired and strung out to let go, and for a while I couldn't figure out why. Then I lay on my couch again and closed my eyes and saw Brad Schale's sneering mug.

That was it—the possibility that Schale was still in town, maybe still in possession of a key to Eric's apartment, next to Nancy Kane's. If Eric made bail, Schale might try to bring him back under his influence, or punish him for not carrying out his mission. I wanted at least to prevent that, maybe even to hunt him down and bring him to justice and get the satisfaction of wiping that ugly sneer off his face.

The phone rang. On the chance that it was Nancy Kane I picked it up. Before I could say anything, I heard, "This is Paul Danner. Karen's dead. Murdered. She was shot at our house in Brookfield. Whoever did it also killed Victoria, our maid."

"When?"

"Earlier today, probably sometime in the morning, but the bodies weren't discovered until a little after noon. The police got through to me in Sheboygan to let me know, and I came right down. When I got here the cops told me what Eric did downtown at the rally, but that's the least of our problems now."

"Where are you?"

"The Police Administration Building. The Brookfield police have two men here. They've been grilling Eric, trying to get a confession out of him. I'm acting as his legal counsel until my lawyer can get down here from his fishing trip in the U.P."

"What's he saying?"

"That he's innocent. He says he has an alibi. He said you saw him at the rally in Marquette Park not long after it started at ten-thirty. The cops say the murders could have happened long enough before then for Eric to have committed them and then driven downtown."

"What Eric said is true. I did see him. Did the cops say why they suspect him?"

"Fritz, our gardener, saw Eric's Explorer pull up to the front of the house sometime between nine thirty and ten this morning, then leave after about fifteen minutes. He was working and assumed it was Eric, so he didn't think anything of it. Later, Fritz went to the back door to consult with Karen about something. When he didn't get a response, he went in and looked around and found the bodies."

"It sounds like he didn't positively ID Eric as the driver."

"He didn't, but try telling that to the cops. I talked to Fritz by phone. He's pretty shaken up. I think he realizes he could have been a victim, too."

"Did he hear gunshots?"

"No. He was on a riding mower and had ear coverings on. Can you come? I'd like you back on the job, working for me. I should have listened to you when you came to me in Madison after Eric returned. I was caught up in the campaign and relieved to have Eric back and wanted to put the whole thing behind us."

"You don't have to hire me to testify that I saw Eric at Marquette Park yesterday morning."

"I know, but I want you to find whoever killed Karen and Victoria and clear Eric's name."

"You sound sure that Eric didn't do it."

"I am."

So was I.

"Why not let the cops handle it?" I said.

"Because they're going to be under pressure to solve this, and it looks like the easiest route to that is through Eric. I'd like you to do some digging of your own and see what you can come up with. I'll pay you, of course, separately from what I paid you before."

"I'll be there as soon as I can."

Twenty minutes later I was parking on the street near the Police Administration Building. I needed rest, a shower, a decent meal, but I was about to get my wish to go hunting for Brad Schale.

CHAPTER 31

Paul Danner was waiting for me outside the building, pacing back and forth and smoking. He looked grim and shaken. Before we went in he told me he had laid the groundwork and got clearance for me to see Eric.

"Maybe you should talk to him without me there," he said. "He might open up better."

"I agree."

Danner said, "Before you see him let me fill you in on a couple of things. The cops warned me that it's not looking good for Eric, especially if a ballistics test shows that the gun they found in his vehicle is the one that was used to kill Karen and Victoria. Also, money and jewelry were taken from the safe. It looks like whoever did this forced Karen to open the safe and then shot her, and probably shot Victoria because she was a witness. The cops found some jewelry in the SUV, but only a few pieces. I haven't been to the house yet, but they said the safe was empty. That means there's plenty more that's unaccounted for. But the cops seem to want to use what they found in the car to build a case against Eric."

"Does Eric know about the jewelry?"

"If he does, he didn't hear it from me. I didn't want him to think I suspected him. The cops talked to him first then let me have some time with him. He said he didn't know anything and that that's what he told them. I think he's holding back, though. I think he's afraid of something. The ordeal he's been through and being accused of murder could account for that, but I sense something else."

"Did Brad Schale's name come up when you talked to him?"

Danner's face registered fear, recognition, and dismay all at once, as if he had just heard an alarm bell and realized at the same moment that he was hearing it too late.

"No."

"I'll see what I can get out of him."

"I'll wait for you."

A cop in uniform escorted me to an interrogation room. A few minutes later another cop brought Eric, in jail coveralls and handcuffs.

"Are the cuffs necessary?" I said to the cop.

"If you're okay with it, we can take them off. I'll be right outside."

"I'm okay with it."

The cop took off the cuffs. My hope was that without them Eric would relax some and be more inclined to open up, but he looked scared, defeated and demoralized. He sat hunched over the table, avoiding eye contact with me.

"Eric," I said, "I was at your house in Brookfield a couple

of days ago. I talked to your step-mom. I know you were there before that to ask her for money and that Brad Schale was with you."

He squirmed in his chair.

"When you went there that day was the door locked?"

"Sure. We always kept the doors locked."

"Did you knock, or did you have your own key and let yourself in?"

"I let myself in with my key. I don't have to knock to get into my own house."

"Where's the key now?"

"I don't know," he said. "I lost it."

"Can you remember the last time you saw it?"

"I guess it was that time I was there, when I went to get the money."

"Why was Brad Schale with you?"

"We were on our way to my apartment from Cudahy. I needed to detour by the house, and he happened to be along." There was a pleading in his voice, as if he didn't expect to be believed.

"Why did he come in the house with you?"

He looked down at his hands then up again. "I don't know. He got out of the car when I did and came up to the house with me. I didn't ask him to or anything, he just did. Maybe he was curious to see where I lived."

"After you got inside what happened?"

"What do you mean what happened?"

"Where was your step-mom?"

"I saw Victoria first, and she went and got her. She asked me what I wanted, and I told her, and she went to the safe and got the money for me."

"Where's the safe?"

"In my dad's office."

"When you left, did Brad Schale ask where the money came from?"

"Maybe."

"Did you tell him?"

"I guess."

"And that was the last time you remember having your key to the house in Brookfield?"

"Yeah."

"Have you told the cops about any of this?"

"No."

"Why not?"

"They didn't ask."

"Did Brad Schale tell you not to say anything about it?" His eyes squirmed with fear.

"I don't want to talk any more."

"There's just one more thing, Eric."

"I didn't kill my step-mom."

"I know that," I said. "Listen to me, Eric. We both know Brad Schale killed your step-mom and Victoria. I know you're afraid of him, and I know why. You're convinced he'll kill you too if you say anything."

He bit his lower lip and looked away. I grabbed his chin and jerked his head around to force him to look me in the eye. "You're right," I said. "He would kill you if he thought you were a threat, or even if you're no longer useful to him. But if you tell me what you know he can be stopped before he gets to you. You're safe as long as you're here in jail. But you have to be honest and you have to be brave."

He nodded tentatively.

"I want you to tell me about this morning, before I saw you at the park," I said. "Where did you start out from? How did you get downtown? Tell me everything you can think of."

"We were in Cudahy," he said. "We stayed there overnight. I left in the morning in the car Brad usually drives. He said he needed my SUV. He didn't say why."

"Didn't you ask him?"

He looked down at his hands again and said, "No. He said to park downtown then call him and let him know where I was, then wait for him there. And I did. Then later he came and we switched vehicles."

"Which parking lot?"

"The one on Clybourn, under 794. It was called Badger something."

"Was there an attendant on duty?"

"Yeah, a black guy."

"Do you think he noticed you switching vehicles with Brad Schale?"

He brightened. "I know he did. The lot was almost full, but we were the only customers there at the time. When Brad came in he didn't park in a space. He just pulled up behind me. We talked for a little bit, then the attendant, the black guy, came over to see what was going on. Then we switched. I backed the car out and he parked my Explorer. He got in the car and took off without paying. I thought I'd have to pay for him, but the black guy didn't say anything."

"What did you talk about before Brad Schale left?"

"He didn't like where I parked. He said I should have gone to the top of a parking garage where we could switch without being seen. But he didn't tell me that before." Eric held his hands palms up, and his voice was pleading. "Then he said I better do what I was supposed to do."

"And if you didn't?"

Eric put his face in his hands and broke down and wept. I opened the door and signaled to the cop that we were finished.

Paul Danner was waiting for me in the lobby. He gave me a look that mixed hope and desperation.

He said, "What do you think?"

"I think we don't have a lot of time. Give me thirty-six hours. If I can't come through by then, odds are I can't come through at all." I almost added *without going back north*, but I didn't want to suggest that that might be an option.

I said, "Whatever you do, don't make bail for Eric. He's safer in jail."

CHAPTER 32

I could have told everything I knew to the cops and handed it over to them, but I didn't because I thought Paul Danner had good reason for not trusting them, because I saw the potential for a messy jurisdictional dispute between Milwaukee and Brookfield, and because I was itching for a shot at Brad Schale myself. For that to happen I needed to get to the parking lot attendant on duty when Eric switched vehicles with Brad Schale, and I needed Brad Schale to stick around a while before heading back north. My guess was that he would stay in the area at least long enough to fence the stolen jewelry. And I had a feeling that he might like to eliminate Eric Danner.

Before going home I went to the parking lot Eric had told me about. I parked on the street and walked up to the kiosk. The attendant, a young white guy, slid open a window. I introduced myself and showed him my license.

"I need to talk to the attendant that was on duty this morning."

"What about?"

"It's a case I'm working on. I want to ask him about two men he may have seen on the lot who switched vehicles."

"What kind of case?"

He seemed to be stalling me.

"Multiple murders. I can appreciate your need to be discreet, but what the attendant saw this morning could prevent an innocent kid from taking the rap."

He gave a slight concessionary nod of the head.

"The guy you want is Henry. He owns this lot. He'll be back tomorrow morning at six o'clock."

"I don't suppose you could give me his home phone and address."

"Sorry."

When I got home it felt like midnight, but it was only seven-thirty. I called Nancy Kane's cell phone. She answered on the second ring.

"Where are you?" I said.

"In my apartment."

"You need to get out. Is there somewhere you can go?"

"Why? What's going on?"

"Brad Schale killed a couple of people this morning and Eric is under suspicion for it. I'm pretty sure Schale has a key to Eric's apartment. I can't think of why he'd show up there, but I'd feel better if you weren't around if he did. You can stay at my place if you need to."

"I've got a friend I can stay with."

She sounded scared. I imagined her with that doe-in-the-headlights look.

"Stay with your friend. If you want me to, I'll come over right now and give you an escort."

"That's okay. I'll be out of here within an hour. Are you sure this is necessary?"

"No, but I'm not sure it isn't. Do you feel like taking the chance?"

"I guess not."

"If Brad Schale shows up before you leave, turn out the lights, lock the door and call me."

Left hanging was whether or not Brad Schale was still in the area. If he wasn't, I'd probably hand things over to the police after all, but I needed to know. I remembered following him to Gladys Eicken's house in Cudahy. I looked her up in the phone book and called her.

A woman answered in a voice quavery with age.

"Hello-o."

"Is Brad Schale there?"

"He's not here right now. I think he and Douglas have gone to Tony's."

That could be a bar or the name of a friend. I took a chance.

"When does Tony's close?"

"I'm not sure. After my bedtime, is all I know."

She sounded like a sweet enough old lady, and if her son and grandson had turned out as they had in spite of her best efforts then I felt for her. But she might be a sweet old lady who also happened to be a rabid Nazi racist.

"I need to talk to Brad. Is that the Tony's on . . . oh, you know."

"That's it. The one on Lake Drive. I don't like Douglas going there—it's kind of a rough place—but what can I do?"

"I understand, ma'am. If I don't catch Brad there, maybe I'll try again tomorrow. Did you say he was going to be around awhile?"

"Well, I'm not sure I did say that, but I believe he will be."

"Thank you, ma'am."

"You're welcome."

I found Tony's Tap in the Yellow Pages at 5475 South Lake Drive in Cudahy. My metro area map indicated that it was across from Warnimont Park.

I considered arming myself and going straight to Tony's right then, but I wasn't sure what I'd be walking into. I needed to do some more groundwork first, and I preferred to get Schale alone, under circumstances that I had more control over.

My next step was to look up notary publics in the Yellow Pages. I'd need one if my visit to Henry, the parking lot attendant, worked out as I hoped it would.

CHAPTER 33

I was too hyped up to read or relax or sleep, so, for diversion, I went to a film at the Oriental Theatre, walking distance from my place. The film featured lots of greed, betrayal, lust, and violence. On the way home I stopped at a coffee shop and spent some time there reading newspapers. The news, the metro pages anyway, was full of greed, betrayal, lust, and violence. I got home around midnight and still couldn't sleep. When I finally did—briefly, fitfully—I dreamed about greed, betrayal, lust, and violence. By the time I awoke the next morning a pattern had taken hold in my mind.

I had a toasted bagel and a short pot of coffee, and was at the parking lot on Clybourn under 794 by nine-thirty. I pulled up to the kiosk, turned off my car and got out. The attendant came over. He was big and brawny with a stern face.

I showed him my license. "I stopped by last night," I said.

"I heard. I'm Henry Alton," he said. "What can I do for you?"

The stern countenance was still in place, but Henry had an air of affability about him.

"I'm looking for information involving a murder case."

"That's serious crime."

"Yes, it is. I'm specifically interested in two guys that were here yesterday morning and switched vehicles. I understand you were on duty."

"That's right."

I showed him the photo of Eric Danner and a print of the shot I took of Brad Schale next to the lake up north.

Henry nodded.

"I remember them, especially the older one for the sneer on his face and the attitude. The younger one came and did kind of an odd thing. Then the other guy came onto the lot. Yeah, they switched vehicles."

"It's that switch that I'm most interested in, but what's the odd thing the younger one did?"

"He came in around eight-forty-five or so in kind of an old, gray Buick. I gave him his ticket. But instead of getting out of his car after he parked, he just sat there. We don't have a rule says you can't do that. I figured he was waiting for somebody. But I kept an eye on him. He made a call on a cell phone.

"Around ten o'clock, the other fella comes in driving a red SUV. He didn't park in a space, just pulled up behind the Buick then got out and sat in the Buick with the first guy. I went over. It looked like they were having an argument. I rapped on the passenger-side window, to give the second guy his ticket—my way of letting him know he needed to park or leave. He got out all aggressive and said he'd only be a couple of minutes, that he was here to switch cars with his friend. He didn't say as much, but it was like he was telling me he didn't have to pay since he wasn't parking. Policy is, you drive onto the lot and there's an empty space, you pay when you leave. I make exceptions all the time. People change their mind or come in looking for directions. But that's just it, *I* make the exceptions. I got the impression he didn't like a black man telling him what to do. They finally made the switch. The first guy parked the SUV where the Buick was, and the other one drove off in the Buick without paying. I didn't challenge him or call the cops or anything. I was glad to see him go. I haven't seen very many people I dislike on sight, but he was one."

"Then what?"

"The younger one took off on foot. After maybe an hour he came back, paid and left.

I showed Henry the photos again.

"You're sure it was these two?"

"I'm sure."

"If you're willing to testify to that, it could prevent an innocent man from taking the rap in the murder case I mentioned."

"Let me guess—the older one's the guilty party and he's trying to frame the younger one."

"That's how it looks. Are you game for this? It could complicate your life. It could even put you at risk."

Henry set his jaw. "If it's the right thing to do, I'll do it."

"If the older guy figures out that what you saw yesterday could unravel his plan, he might come looking for you."

Henry smiled. "Would you want to mess with me?"

Indeed I wouldn't. He was much bigger and stronger than me, well over six feet and built like a defensive end. His size advantage over Brad Schale would be even more daunting.

"No," I said. "Neither would the killer. If he wants to take you out he'll come armed and try to blow you away before you can close ranks with him. No Marquis of Queensbury."

Henry shook his head and smiled with perfect confidence.

"I keep a piece here in my office," he said. "And I've dealt with plenty of bad characters. I appreciate your concern, but I got a family—wife, a kid in college and one close to it—and I'm not letting a punk like him disrupt my business."

I admired Henry, but I was concerned that his confidence didn't quite take into account the possibilities posed by a well-armed sociopath. But his willingness to cooperate served my purpose, and he seemed determined, so I didn't press any harder.

I said, "If you're ready, we can do this right now."

"Let's do it."

I went to my car and got a yellow legal pad I had brought with me.

I said to Henry, "I'd like you to write out a condensed version of what you just told me about the switch, with reference to these photos. I put names on the back. While you're doing that I'll make a phone call."

Henry went into the kiosk and got to work. I used my cell phone to call the number of the Arthur Brown Mobile Notary Public service that I had looked up the night before. Arthur Brown said he'd be right over.

Henry finished and showed me what he had written. It was clear and concise and covered the essential points. As we waited for Arthur Brown to show, Henry treated me to a cup of coffee. It was righteous stuff, and we spent our time comparing notes on the Brewers and the Bucks.

A few minutes later, Arthur Brown's van pulled into the lot. A guy in glasses got out wearing a white short-sleeve shirt and a polyester tie with a knot the size of my fist.

"Here's the deal," I said to him. "Mr. Henry Alton here has written a statement and we want you to witness his signing it."

"Can I see the statement?"

He read it then asked Henry for a photo ID. Henry produced his drivers license. Arthur Brown told Henry to sign. Henry did, and Arthur Brown affixed his seal and signed.

I put the legal pad and the photos in a large manila envelope that I had brought. I licked and sealed the tab and bent down the two wings of the metal clip and put the envelope in my car. I paid Arthur Brown with cash. He left. Henry didn't charge him for his time on the lot. When I offered to pay for him he waved it off.

I gave Henry one of my business cards.

"This is if you need to get hold of me for some reason. Thanks for your help, Henry. And watch your back."

Henry said, "If you need anything else, you know where to find me."

So does Brad Schale, I thought.

I said, "What do I owe you?"

"A cup of coffee."

We shook hands.

"I'm good for it."

CHAPTER 34

My bounty hunter blood was up, but I still had to figure out how to maneuver Brad Schale into position and bring him in. In part to simplify things, I dismissed the idea that he'd go to Eric's apartment. That left Cudahy—the house and Tony's. I drove off for Cudahy.

I went by the house first. The gray Buick wasn't on the street. I drove to Tony's Tap. It was set into a residential neighborhood, insulated from it by a tall fence made of vertical boards. It was still morning, but some trucks and Harleys were in the lot. I pulled into a small parking space in Warnimont Park across Lake Drive and watched for a while. Two guys came in a pickup with a Confederate flag decal on the rear window and went in. They didn't look like the type that shared the cooking and housework with the wife.

I couldn't decide if I wanted to stake out until Schale

appeared, or to go back and forth between the house and Tony's until I spotted his car. Either way, I might not come across him alone and under circumstances that were to my advantage, and that was what I wanted. And to get it I'd need some kind of bait.

I returned to the Eicken house. The gray Buick still wasn't on the street. I drove by Tony's again. No Buick. I decided to try Eric's apartment after all. On the way I could drive by Henry's and check on things there.

It took me fifteen minutes to get to the lot on Clybourn. I could see the bubble lights on the cop cars from a block away. An ambulance sped past me going in the other direction, without lights and siren. I drove onto the lot. A cop in uniform approached me and told me that I had entered a crime scene and would have to leave.

"What's going on, officer? Where's Henry?" I thought I already knew the answer.

I showed him my license. He gave it a long look.

"We found your business card on his desk. I think you should tell me what your connection is."

"I was here this morning talking to Henry about a case I'm working on. Where's Henry?"

"He's on his way to the morgue. Somebody shot him."

"How long ago?"

"Less than an hour, we think. A customer drove in to park, and when nobody came out he looked and found him on the floor of the shed with four slugs in him and called it in."

"Any witnesses?"

The cop shook his head.

"We're checking the area and the buildings nearby. So far nothing. And nobody's come to us off the street. I have a feeling we're going to need to get lucky on this one."

I left, numb with anger and frustration. Henry had been adamant about not abandoning his post and about his ability to handle things himself. Still, I felt partially implicated in his death.

I went to my office and spent some time stewing and pacing. Then it came to me—the bait. I called the house in Cudahy again.

The old woman answered.

"Mrs. Eicken?"

"Ye-es."

"Is Brad Schale there?"

I was hoping the answer would be no and that she wouldn't recognize my voice from the day before.

"No, he isn't."

"Can you give him a message for me when he comes back?"

"I sure can."

"This is Eric Danner. Please tell him that I'm out on bail and that I need to talk to him. I'd like to meet him at Tony's at ten o'clock tonight. And it might be better if he came alone. It's pretty important."

"I'll tell him. Tony's at ten o'clock."

"Right. Alone if possible."

"Is this the Eric that's been here?"

"Yes, ma'am."

"Out on bail, you say. I hope you're not in trouble."

"Me too, ma'am. Thanks. Bye."

"You're welcome. Bye, now."

CHAPTER 35

When the time came for me to make my move I carried my .38 in a shoulder holster under a light jacket, the Browning and its extra clip in a side pocket—seventeen shots in all—and a set of plastic zip-tie handcuffs in the other pocket. I went south on 794, east on Layton Avenue into Cudahy all the way to Lake Drive, and worked my way down.

I sat across from Tony's in Warnimont Park and watched. Only a few cars were on the lot. I was counting on Gladys Eicken's having accurately conveyed the message to Brad Schale and on Schale's coming alone, but I was determined to act no matter what.

Schale was on time. He pulled into the lot in the gray Buick and parked up against the fence at the far end. He got out and looked around. He was alone and appeared to have taken the bait.

I put my car in gear and crossed Lake Drive and entered the lot. I drove right past him without his noticing me. I suppose since I wasn't driving a red Ford Explorer he paid me no mind. I parked behind Schale's car, blocking it, and got out.

Schale was in a pool of light made by neon beer signs in Tony's front window. I came up from behind him.

"Brad Schale, game's up."

He turned and looked at me, then past me.

"You're blocking my car," he said.

I walked toward him and entered the pool of light. He recognized me.

"What the . . ."

I pulled the .38 out of my shoulder holster and pointed it at him.

"You don't need your car. You're coming with me."

"You think so?"

"Yes I do. Before you killed Henry Alton, the owner of that parking lot, I got a signed testimony from him in which he says he witnessed the switch of vehicles you pulled with Eric Danner yesterday. That implicates you in two murders. And it shouldn't be too hard to pin Henry's murder on you, too."

With a kind of clumsy quickness, Schale crouched and scrambled to the far side of a pickup, leaving three or four vehicles between him and me. He popped up next to the bed and fired two shots at me, missing with both. I crouched down next to a car and moved to the front end of it, nearest the building.

A guy poked his head out of Tony's entrance. Schale fired wildly in his direction, and he ducked back inside. It was an amazingly stupid move on Schale's part, and a waste of a bullet.

Still in a crouch, I went down the line of parked vehicles

until I flanked him and drove him out into the open with a shot that ripped into a door panel near his head. There were no cars on the other side of the lot to provide cover, so he ran out of the lot, across Lake Drive and into Warnimont Park.

I went after him. At the edge of the park, he turned on the run and fired in my direction. The shot nicked me on the outside of my left thigh, enough to slow me down, but not much.

He moved into a stand of trees. I followed, firing once to cover my approach. I was counting shots. That made four for him, two for me.

I moved toward him from tree to tree to draw his fire. It worked. A bullet thudded into a tree in front of me. I tried it again. The hammer of his gun clacked on an empty chamber. He was either using a five-shot, like mine, or he hadn't fully loaded his gun.

I got the Browning out and fired to keep him in place until I flanked him as I had in the parking lot. He ran into the open. I fired twice at the ground near his feet. He stopped. I came out of the trees. We were no more than ten feet apart, with open space between us. The moon hung high in a clear sky, almost full. Beyond the bluff, it shimmered on Lake Michigan. I put the Browning in a jacket pocket and held the .38 on him.

In outline under the moon, Schale looked like one of the targets I shot at on the practice range. He lowered his gun to his side and dropped it, raised his hands up next to his ears in a gesture of surrender, and smirked. He must have figured he had denied me the satisfaction of shooting him, now that he was unarmed. Under different circumstances that might have been the case, but my judgment was skewed by the cumulative effect of the events of the last few weeks, especially the last couple of days.

At least that's what I told myself as I emptied my .38 on him—two in the chest, and one in the mouth to wipe off the smirk.

He crumpled and died.

I stood over him.

Back across Lake Drive a squad car pulled into Tony's with lights and siren. I limped toward it under the light of the moon.

EPILOGUE

Jill was off her game, and I thought I knew why. Nancy Kane's disingenuous charm and sweet good looks were making her urban sophistication and irony seem jaded, stale, and weary.

She had invited me to join the *Journal Sentinel* Friday night happy-hour crowd at Delaney's. We were around a long table— me, Jill, Terrell (without The Oak), some others from the *Journal Sentinel*, and Nancy Kane, whom I had taken the liberty to ask without telling Jill. I didn't know if that was Nancy's scene or not, but I wanted to celebrate our collaboration of sorts in the Eric Danner case, and she was handling her beer with the best of us. Jill also might have been wondering if something was going on between me and Nancy.

Part of me was enjoying Jill's discomfiture, but I was off my game too and not enjoying much else. For one thing, my leg hurt where Brad Schale's bullet nicked me. I had dismissed the wound as superficial and dressed it myself without going for medical attention, but was beginning to wonder if that was a mistake. And my mind was drifting back and forth from Delaney's to that bluff above Lake Michigan in the moonlight, and to what awaited me in the confessional—having to own up to my killing of Brad Schale and to the lie I told the Cudahy cops about shooting him in self-defense. Two beers into happy hour, I thought of that act in terms of the word *murder* for the first time—premeditated murder, if I were to be honest about my mindset while loading my guns before taking off for Cudahy. Mortal sin. I knew there were no limits to the confidentiality of the confessional, but I couldn't shake the feeling that my case might be an exception.

Then Andy Matuszak came over. He was there with some cop friends, and I thought he only wanted to join us for a round, but he pulled up a chair next to me, and when I turned to greet him he gave me a penetrating look, as if he was reading my mind. With so many of us at that long table, multiple conversations were going on at once. Andy had my right ear to himself, and said to me discreetly, "I was planning to use Brad Schale as bait to land bigger fish. I told you that."

In an attempt to deflect Andy and to change the subject, I said to Nancy Kane, "Nancy, I've yet to hear you say what you told Eric Danner by cell phone to get him down off that scaffolding."

Nancy said, "I merely pointed out that his threat to jump was no threat at all, since from where he was perched he'd go straight into the Milwaukee River. I told him he wouldn't drown, or even get hurt. Instead, he'd get hauled out like a fish and taken away in handcuffs. I asked him if he wanted to end up not only in more trouble than he already was in, but also suffer the embarrassment of being soaking wet on the evening news."

"Brilliant," I said.

In my peripheral vision, I could see that Andy was still there.

"Maybe," Nancy said. "To be honest, it looked to me like if he didn't push off hard enough he could have landed short and broken his neck and killed himself after all." She shrugged. "Anyway, he bought it, which was what I was hoping for."

At which point Jill, who had been having difficulty finding a place to join the conversation, said, "Not only the evening news, sweetie, but the front page of the next day's paper as well. Some people *do* still read newspapers, you know."

The remark was so clumsy that it brought conversation to a halt for a moment, at least at our end of the table. Jill suddenly had to use the ladies' room.

Terrell raised a glass to Nancy Kane's quick thinking and insight. I raised mine, clinked it to Terrell's and some others and drank, but in my mind I was back in Cudahy, facing Brad Schale in the moonlight, his gun out of bullets on the ground, then emptying my .38 on him.

I stood over him.

In my past imaginings, such an act perpetrated on one such as Schale was cathartic and satisfying. In the event, it was cathartic—some, anyway, for a brief moment—but far from satisfying. It felt mostly gratuitous, beastly and brutish.

I settled back in my chair again. Andy hadn't gone away. Leaning close to my ear, he said, "I talked to a cop in Cudahy that's on that task force I told you about. He said Schale's gun was empty."

"Sure," I said. "He emptied it trying to kill me."

Andy gave me a narrow look.

I stood over him. Schale's teeth were splattered in the grass and there was a messy exit wound in the back of his head.

In a booth across the way, a priest I had seen celebrate mass a few times at St. John's Cathedral was drinking beer with some friends. They were laughing.

Jill returned. I considered what she'd say if she knew of my dread at the prospect of opening the dark inner chambers of my dark heart in the confessional. *Then don't.* So much easier. So tempting.

"We'll talk," Andy said, and left my side and rejoined his cop friends.

The priest got up, took leave of his companions and headed for the door. I stood and intercepted him and put a hand on his arm. He stopped and turned to me, earnest and curious.

I stood over him . . . and sneered.

"Father, will you hear my confession?"